C0-ATW-267

JAKE LOGAN

SLOCUM
ON GHOST MESA

J

JOVE BOOKS, NEW YORK

SLOCUM ON GHOST MESA

A Jove Book / published by arrangement with
the author

PRINTING HISTORY
Jove edition / August 2001

All rights reserved.
Copyright © 2001 by Penguin Putnam Inc.
This book, or parts thereof, may not be reproduced in any form
without permission.
For information address: The Berkley Publishing Group,
a division of Penguin Putnam Inc.,
375 Hudson Street, New York, New York 10014.

The Penguin Putnam Inc. World Wide Web site address is
www.penguinputnam.com

ISBN: 0-515-13116-4

A JOVE BOOK®
Jove Books are published by The Berkley Publishing Group,
a division of Penguin Putnam Inc.,
375 Hudson Street, New York, New York 10014.
JOVE and the "J" design
are trademarks belonging to Penguin Putnam Inc.

PRINTED IN THE UNITED STATES OF AMERICA

10 9 8 7 6 5 4 3 2 1

SIX-GUN SENSE

"Drop your hardware," Slocum ordered. His Winchester roved restlessly from one outlaw to another. He thought he had them treed. He was wrong.

The quiet one at the fire went for his six-gun. Slocum saw the movement from the corner of his eye, went into a crouch, swiveled and fired in a smooth action. The robber's bullet went into the ground; Slocum's rifle bullet went into the man's chest.

The robber gasped, started to reach for the wound and then realized he was dead. He slumped to the ground, the six-shooter falling from his nerveless fingers.

The other two robbers weren't inclined to shoot it out with Slocum, but they both turned into rabbits and hightailed it. Slocum took careful aim and fired at one man. He stumbled, went to his knees and then flopped onto his back like a fish out of water.

"You shot me!" he shrieked. "You got me in the leg!"

"You don't shut up, I'll put you out of your misery for good," Slocum said, laying his rifle down away from the wounded man's reach.

1

The buzzard flew high, its ugly head in heaven and its sharp eyes fixed on hell below. It spread its powerful wings wider and wheeled sharply when a blast of rising hot air from the desert gave it additional lift. It dipped lower as it studied the burning, arid terrain for any hint of a decent rotting meal. Barring that, the double-rutted road through the alkali plain sometimes offered up a tasty tidbit waiting to die.

Not today. Not at the moment. But soon. It was always that way.

The buzzard circled and rode the air currents higher, heading over the nearby steep-sided mesa. Dashing amid the graves closed to it by rocks and the religious determination of the Paiute Indians, the buzzard spotted small rodents hardly worth going after. They were quick, and ventured out in the heat of the day for only minutes before ducking back into the cool depths of their burrows. The buzzard hunted on, hoping to find a meal. It had been almost three days since it had ripped apart the coyote that had died of thirst.

Away from the barren mesa it flew, a distant billowing dust cloud catching its sharp gaze. The best source of food it had ever found approached.

Humans.

It would dine. Soon. Again.

John Slocum rocked to and fro in the stagecoach, trying to doze but finding it impossible. The furnacelike heat boiling in through the windows hit him like repeated punches to his face. He had argued with the two men sitting across from him about lowering the canvas flaps over the stage's open windows. The canvas would block out the choking clouds of dust kicked up from the wheels, and seemingly funneled directly to Slocum's face. But they had both argued how lowering the canvas window shades would make it even hotter inside, so he had backed off.

Slocum wiped away some of the grit on his face, now mixed with sweat. He felt dirty all over and more irritable than when he had given in to the two men.

"Stop fidgeting," growled the man across from him. "You're makin' a racket that'd wake the dead."

"Must work," said the other man, looking as if he would scream at any instant. From the way he dressed in threadbare clothing that might once have been costly duds, Slocum pegged him as a traveling salesman down on his luck. "We're all awake. Since we are damned and on our way to perdition, that means we're dead and don't know it yet. And that—"

"Shut up," snapped the man opposite Slocum. "Say another word and I'll make damn sure you die right here on the spot."

"Please, gentlemen," came the insistent words from Slocum's right. He shifted a mite on the hard stagecoach bench and tried not to stare at the dark-haired woman. In spite of the dust and heat, she looked almost as fresh as a daisy. Her long patrician nose wrinkled as a new cloud of brown grit gusted through the compartment, but she tried to ignore it, save for a tiny ineffectual movement with a linen handkerchief across her bow-shaped ruby lips. She dressed tastefully enough, but not expensively. Sensing Slocum's interest in her, she turned bright blue eyes to him that bored through to the bottom of his soul.

"Sorry, ma'am," he said. "I didn't mean to stare. It's just that the view's better in your direction than anywhere else." Slocum tilted his head slightly to indicate the two men opposite him in the stage.

The woman smiled just enough to encourage him. Travel had been arduous across from Laramie, with nothing worth staring at outside the stagecoach. Conversation was always difficult over the rattle and creak of the stagecoach, but Slocum thought he might pursue it with the raven-tressed beauty now that they had, it seemed, established a common dislike for the other two passengers.

"The trip is wearing all our nerves to a frazzle," she said. "Behave." The sharp edge in her command brought Slocum up short. She stared directly at the man across from Slocum, as if she knew him and was comfortable ordering him around. This surprised Slocum since the woman had not appeared to know any of the men when she had boarded the stage.

"It'd be a damned sight easier keepin' my temper if I could throw him out," the man said, poking his traveling companion in the ribs with a sharp elbow.

Slocum rocked to his feet and grabbed the salesman's wrist before he could whip out a wicked, short-bladed knife from a sheath in his boot and stick it in his attacker's belly.

"The heat's riling us all," Slocum said, keeping his grip until the salesman settled back, letting the knife slip back into his boot top. Slocum glared at the other man for inciting the salesman, then sank back amid a new cloud of blinding dust blowing through the windows. No matter how he turned, he could not keep out of the grit.

He decided it no longer mattered to him if the others in the coach were happy with his decisions. Any more dirt in his face and he might kill both men out of sheer exasperation. Slocum reached outside and caught at the strings holding up the canvas curtains. A quick tug released the knots and brought the flaps down.

"Hey, I tol' you not to do that." The man across from Slocum jerked as if he had been shot.

"Afraid of the dark?" the salesman jibed. "Of course you are since we're all going to die alone and in the dark!"

"Shut *up*!" roared the man as he grabbed for the salesman again.

Slocum was caught off balance when the stagecoach lurched and something slammed him hard across the interior. He found himself with an armful of delightful, wiggling femininity. A hint of perfume clung to her tousled hair, which momentarily drove away the stench of sweat and filth. Slocum had no chance to appreciate his position because the stage lurched in the other direction. This time a sick cracking sound echoed across the desert and the stagecoach sank to the ground.

Slocum heard the driver swearing and jerking hard at the reins to keep the team from dragging the now immobile coach along. The compartment came to a halt, tilted at a crazy angle. Again Slocum was not inclined to complain too much. The dark-haired beauty had flopped on top of him and struggled enough to show her heart wasn't really in getting away.

"You'd better get off him," snarled the man who had been seated across from Slocum. The woman muttered something, and then Slocum felt feet and arms poking into him as the other passengers disentangled themselves.

"We are all doomed," moaned the salesman.

"The axle broke, that's all," Slocum said. He had heard the crack of wood before and knew they were in for long hot hours waiting for the next stage to come by and rescue them. From what he had seen of the stage's cargo stowed in the boot behind the compartment and on the roof, they didn't have a spare axle.

What stage ever carried one?

Slocum heaved himself upright enough to pull himself out the door. The stagecoach canted at a thirty-degree angle at the side of the road while the horses neighed and danced and complained bitterly in their harnesses. The driver hopped down and began unhooking the horses to keep them from hurting themselves.

"We're stranded for a spell," said the woman, heaving a deep sigh as she studied the rear of the coach. She saw what Slocum had already determined: the axle was broken.

"Hell 'n damnation," growled the driver, hunkering down and running a callused hand over the busted wood. "How'm I supposed to fix this?"

"You'll have to wait for the next stage," Slocum said, "unless you have some way of fixing it."

"I ain't no wheelwright," the driver said. He edged away, stood and then spat. The glob of tobacco sizzled when it hit a rock. "I don't rightly know when the next stage'll come by either."

"We've got horses," Slocum said. "We can ride into Hard Rock."

"And leave the strongbox? Mister, they'd skin me alive if I tried that."

"Who'd steal it out here?" Slocum squinted as he studied the barren land. High above circled a solitary buzzard, waiting for something to die. He wished it were within range of his Colt Navy. He would blow the accursed carrion eater from the sky.

"I got my orders," the driver said. "You ain't from 'round here. We got a passel of real nasty road agents working this stretch of country. You wouldn't believe how many stages don't make it. Why, they must be the orneriest critters on earth, them road agents. They stopped one stagecoach and gunned down one passenger, then let us go."

"Just one?" asked Slocum. "They didn't rob you?"

"Well, shore, they did. But they rode up, gunned down this fellow. A mining engineer headin' back to Laramie, he claimed. Robbed us and off they went. Mean sonsabitches. 'Cuse my French, ma'am," the driver said, smiling in the dark-haired woman's direction.

Slocum wished he could see a few robbers. They might have water. Already his mouth was turning to cotton, and he had been out in the sun for only a few minutes.

"We need to get to shade."

"We're going to die," sobbed the salesman. "It is written. We will all die for our sins!"

Slocum grabbed the other man's arm to prevent him from delivering a fist to the middle of the peddler's face.

"I told you to back off once before. I won't tell you again. Let him be."

"You don't give me orders." The man jerked free of Slocum's grip, stepped back and pushed his coat away from his six-shooter. "Anytime you think you can take me, go for your smoke wagon."

Slocum pegged the man as a petty crook with an inflated opinion of himself and his gunslinging abilities. The man's fingers curled and uncurled, showing how nervous he was—or how eager. Either way, it gave Slocum an edge if he wanted to answer the challenge.

The woman stepped between them. She looked at Slocum, but he had the feeling her words were directed pointedly at the would-be gunfighter.

"We can't afford to fight among ourselves. Survival is more important."

"Yes, ma'am," Slocum said. He couldn't figure out if she knew the other man or if she was as irritated with him as Slocum was. Whatever it was, the man relaxed and backed off.

"We're not finished," the man called before moving away with a sullen look.

"Let him go, sir," she said, her hand warm on Slocum's arm.

"My name's John Slocum, and you're the only sensible one on this stagecoach."

"The only *other* one," she said, smiling brightly. "I'm Jacqueline Renard. Pleased to make your acquaintance."

Slocum and Jacqueline moved away from the coach, letting the driver and peddler argue over how long it would take for them all to die. Slocum couldn't help looking to the bright blue Wyoming sky and seeing the buzzard watching them intently. It had come close to getting a meal. Slocum would have left the other man dead, a bullet through his vile heart.

"What brings you to this desolate land?" Slocum asked. The only real diversion, other than Jacqueline, was a steep-sided mesa a few miles off the road. Lumpy mountains around it hinted at taller mountains in the direction of the town of Hard Rock, but otherwise Slocum knew they were in for a boring time of it.

"The same as you, Mr. Slocum. Opportunity."

"How's that?"

"Aren't you a hard rock miner? You certainly have the muscles." She eyed him appreciatively and the tip of her tongue snaked around her lips, wetting them slightly.

"What opportunity are you expecting to find in Hard Rock?" he asked, changing the subject. Slocum had no real destination in mind, other than heading for the continually moving sunset. He wouldn't know what he hunted for until he found it, and after so many years, he knew that might be never. Laramie had not held him for longer than a week before he grew restless and decided to head for the Pacific coast. He left nothing behind, and what he went to might not be any more thrilling. But he had to find out for himself.

"Not as a miner," Jacqueline said, laughing.

Before Slocum could find out what drew her to the boomtown, gunshots spun him around. His hand flashed to the ebony handle of the six-shooter in its cross-draw holster, but Slocum did not draw.

"It's that peddler," Jacqueline said. "He's gone completely crazy and is shooting at shadows."

"There aren't any shadows," Slocum said in disgust. But the woman was right. The salesman had drawn a small hideout pistol Slocum had not seen and was waving it around. The other passenger dived for cover rather than go after him again. Slocum had saved the man once from the salesman's knife. It looked as if he had to do it again, this time from a wildly waving five-shooter.

He shoved Jacqueline behind him and hurried toward the wild-eyed salesman. Whether heat or something else had driven the man crazy didn't interest Slocum as much as getting the gun from his hand. Slocum feinted, pointed and got the peddler's attention fixed on the high-flying buzzard for the brief instant it took to swing and connect with the point of the man's chin. The salesman's knees turned to water, and he sank to the ground, unconscious.

"Shoulda plugged the varmint," complained the driver, coming out from under the stagecoach. He dragged a battered Winchester with him.

"Gone mad from the heat and boredom," Slocum said, kicking the salesman's gun away. "Get him under the stage where it's cooler."

"How long are we going to have to stay here?" demanded the other man.

"Shut yer tater trap," the driver ordered. The man bristled but saw that Slocum backed up the driver and subsided. "We cain't rightly fix the coach, so we wait. Another stage will be along sometime before noon tomorrow."

"Noon!"

Slocum glared at the complaining man, who stalked off to sit in the dubious shade of a stunted greasewood bush.

"We might as well make the most of our time," Jacqueline said equitably, rummaging through the boot and finding blankets for everyone. While she laid out their bedrolls, Slocum gathered dried brush for a fire. The small amount of provisions came from Slocum's larder, but he did not mind sharing what he had, especially with a woman as lovely as Jacqueline.

Any ideas he had that she had taken a shine to him faded when she pointedly moved her bedroll away from him and closer to the other man, leaving the salesman between them. Slocum shrugged it off. This was hardly the time or place to strike up a romance.

The burning sun dipped behind the nearby mesa, leaving bloody rays behind for long minutes until these too evaporated and turned the land inky with darkness. Slocum lay back on his blanket, stared at the stars as they popped out one by one into the night sky and slowly drifted to sleep, only to come alert less than an hour later when he heard boots crunching in the dry alkali sand.

He sat up, his hand on his six-gun. Jacqueline slept peacefully a few yards away and beyond her wrapped tightly in his blanket lay the other passenger. The driver was propped in the driver's box and snored loudly. The only one missing was the salesman.

Slocum got to his feet and headed toward the darkly looming mesa, knowing the peddler's excursion into the desert might be innocent enough. They had had too little to drink, but the man might have to take a piss. That idea vanished when the salesman let out a cry of stark terror and started shooting.

"Damnation," grunted Slocum, stumbling in the dark as he headed for the spot where he saw the man's silhouette writhing about. He got to his feet and rushed forward, not wanting the reckless spray of lead to hit him. The peddler was crazier than he ought to be from only the heat. He ought to be locked up in an asylum for his own and everyone else's protection.

"Go away, get away!" the peddler screamed. He thrashed about, as if caught in a cloud of invisible gnats. His arms windmilled, and he ducked his head as he plunged into the night, heading for the mesa.

"Calm down," Slocum shouted. "Stop shooting! There's nothing out there!"

A bullet whizzed past him, forcing Slocum to flop belly-down on the ground. He heard the peddler's shrieks of terror. And there was more. He heard the man reloading his gun. He might be mad as a hatter but still had enough sense to be able to reload his pistol.

Slocum froze when he heard something more. He had lived in the wilderness most of his life and thought he had heard every possible sound made by man and beast. But this was unlike anything he had ever heard before. Not a whistle, not a whine, it was a combination, as if wind blew through rock. But he heard words, faint, barely intelligible, in that eerie wail. It was as if someone tried to tell of death and dying but could not.

The salesman began firing again.

"Get away! I won't let you take me. I want to die, but you can't have my soul!" The pistol spat repeatedly. Slocum tried to count and was not sure if he heard five shots or if echoes confused him. Risking it, he got his feet under him and sprinted forward.

The peddler stood at the base of the mesa, his gun aimed upward as he screamed incoherently.

Slocum's eyes followed the line of the man's aim. He stopped dead in his tracks, wondering what was happening. White puffs of steam darted in and out of the jagged rocks on the side of the mesa, looking like snow at times and then vanishing entirely. Once, the cloudy shape firmed and reached out as a bone-chilling whine echoed across the desert.

"Look out!" Slocum shouted, the words torn from his throat. His warning fell on deaf ears. The salesman fired repeatedly, his five-shooter's hammer falling on empty cylinders. Then he screeched as the white mist enveloped him. He dropped his gun, threw his arms over his face as if he could protect himself in this fashion. Then a sound came from the man's throat that was so unearthly it chilled Slocum through and through.

Slocum whipped out his Colt and fired. The bullet blasted through the mist enveloping the peddler, to no avail. For a moment, the white cloud swirled and then evaporated faster than dewdrops under the hot noonday sun. He rushed forward and knelt by the salesman. The man lay flat on his back with a look of extreme terror etched on his face.

On his dead face.

He had died of fright.

2

"Dangest thing I ever did see," mused the stagecoach driver, staring at the salesman's dead body. He looked up at Slocum. "You sure you didn't help this gent along to the Promised Land, just a wee bit?"

"I don't know what killed him," Slocum said. "Might have been fright."

The driver snorted, as if this were the dumbest thing he had ever heard.

"Reckon we got to bury him. I ain't lettin' him rot in the sun 'til the next stage comes along. Can't stand the smell." The driver jerked his thumb upward toward the starry nighttime sky. "Buzzards'll eat too good if we don't do something, and I ain't got a shovel."

"We can cover him with rocks." Slocum spun, hand going to his six-shooter when he heard movement behind him. After finding the peddler dead, Slocum had alerted the driver. No stage company appreciated losing a passenger, especially in such a bizarre fashion. Both Jacqueline Renard and the other passenger had slept through the tumult—until now.

"What's going on?" the man demanded, shoving past Slocum to look at the body.

"Nuthin' you can do a danged thing about," the driver said, " 'less you want to help stack rocks on a dead body."

"He . . . he looks so strange," Jacqueline said, moving up to stare at the body. "So frightened."

"He might have died of a heart attack," Slocum said. He didn't bother telling them about the drifting white mist that had enveloped the salesman seconds before he died. It might have been nothing more than a trick played on his vision by the desert. Heat in the day brought mirages. At night, why not hallucinations? Slocum had heard eating Jimson weed seeds would make a man go out of his head seeing things that weren't there.

"I didn't pay passage to bury a coyote who tried to shoot me," the other passenger said.

"Look, mister," Slocum said. "Nobody's told you to do anything—until now. Go back to the stage and wait."

"You're not ordering me to do anything. Nobody pushes Clay Chettum around!"

"Go back to the stagecoach," Jacqueline said in her sharp voice. Chettum sucked in his breath, let it out in a rush and left without another word. Again Slocum was startled at the way the woman commanded Chettum and the way he obeyed so meekly.

Slocum looked at the driver, who wiped his hands on his pant legs before getting down to the chore of burying the peddler.

"Go on back with Chettum," Slocum said to Jacqueline. "We'll take care of this."

"That's right, missy. We'll do what has to be done. Try to get some beauty sleep, as if you need it." The driver leered, but Jacqueline didn't notice. She stared at the peddler in something approaching amazement. Slocum had figured the sight of a corpse might spook her, but it didn't. If anything, it fascinated her.

Jacqueline left the men to their work. A half hour later

Slocum stepped away and studied the mound of rocks over the salesman's body.

"Think this will do?" Slocum asked.

"Hell, no," the driver said, wiping his hands again. "The coyotes are real hungry this year. Been dry. Might even see a vulture or two peckin' at the rocks to get at what's underneath, but I ain't spendin' more time here to add more to the pile." The driver walked away, muttering to himself about inconsiderate passengers dying during his stage run.

Slocum hung back, wondering what lay atop the mesa looming nearby. Whatever had engulfed the peddler had come from the rocks at the base of the mesa. His green eyes worked up from the darkness at the base all the way to the ragged edge outlined by stars. He blinked when he thought he saw movement on the rim of the mesa. Whatever he saw—or thought he had seen—was gone when he focused more.

He trailed the driver back to the stagecoach. Chettum was asleep again, as was Jacqueline. Slocum started to strike up a conversation with the driver when a mournful howl echoed through the night. The driver clutched his rifle like a lover and curled up, folding himself into a tight ball protected by the driver's box. Talk was the last thing he wanted. Slocum gave up and pulled his blanket around him, falling into fitful sleep with the unearthly wails in his ears.

A little before dawn, Slocum rolled over and banged his hand into a rock. He grumbled and sat up, still more asleep than awake. This changed fast when he realized something was wrong.

Looking around, he saw Chettum still wrapped in his blanket. The driver sawed wood noisily in the box, but there was no trace of Jacqueline Renard anywhere. Slocum got to his feet, wondering if she had wandered off to answer a call of nature. If so, she was in danger. He had spent his life listening to night sounds, and he could not identify what had been howling in the darkness.

Slocum saw the woman's tracks leading in the direction of the mesa, but he quickly lost them on a rocky patch.

"What's got you so riled?" asked the driver, wiping the sleep from his eyes. Slocum reacted, then relaxed.

"Miss Renard's gone." Slocum noted the wind blew fitfully. From the condition of her tracks, if the wind had not blown any stronger than this, she had been gone for more than an hour.

"I ain't waitin' around for her, no, sirree," the driver declared firmly. "Don't care if they lift my scalp at the company office. Losin' one passenger's bad enough, losin' two's worse, but I ain't losin' *my* life, too. Old Gus's ma didn't raise no fools."

"We don't know she's dead," Slocum pointed out.

"And we don't know why she left camp." Old Gus cocked his head to one side, then smiled, showing a broken front tooth. "Hear that? The next stage's on its way. Yipeee!" He jumped in the air, clicked his heels and hit the ground running for the stage. The driver climbed to the top of the tilted stagecoach and began waving to flag down the other stage.

Slocum looked from the road where a dust cloud marked the arrival of the other stagecoach and then to the mesa, now shining like silver in the early morning sun.

Something about the soaring rock spire held Slocum's attention, and it had nothing to do with wondering how the peddler had died. Or where Jacqueline might have gone.

"Get your gear, gents. We'll be in Hard Rock by noon."

"I'm not leaving Miss Renard," Slocum said.

"That's on your head, then," Old Gus said. "Don't care if I show up three passengers short, as long as I have a throat to swallow some whiskey at the Digging Fool Saloon. That gin mill's got the sweetest lookin' lady runnin' it you ever set eyes on."

Slocum hitched up his gun belt and wondered if he should take his rifle. He chose instead to take the burlap desert bag slung on the side of the stagecoach. Water meant more than firepower from the rifle.

"Where you going?" demanded Clay Chettum, finally roused by the clamor put up by the driver.

"He's chasin' after that purty lady."

"What?" This brought Chettum to his feet.

"Miss Renard vanished during the night," Slocum explained. He saw Chettum taking in everything—the approaching stage, the way the driver hooted and hollered and Slocum's determination. What Chettum said next brought Slocum yet another surprise.

"We can't just leave her. If you go after her, I'll come along."

"Suit yourself," Slocum said. He slung the water bag over his shoulder and set off, not bothering to wait for the stage. Clay Chettum hurried to catch up with him.

"Look, Slocum," the man said, "we got off on the wrong foot."

"The heat gets to everyone," Slocum said, his keen eyes sweeping back and forth for any trace of Jacqueline's tracks. Small depressions that might have come from her shoes led him inexorably toward the mesa where the peddler had died from fright the night before.

"Why do you think she took off like this?" Chettum asked. "I mean, she was safe by the stagecoach."

"Can't say," Slocum said, concentrating on the trail. He had quickly dismissed the notion Jacqueline might have been taken from camp forcibly. Nowhere did he see any sign of other men—or even animals. She had left on her own and had not bothered telling anyone. That upset Slocum most of all. What had lured her away?

"There's the grave," Chettum said, pointing to the peddler's cairn. The sun had been up for less than an hour and already coyotes had pawed away a section of the stones, in their still-futile attempt to reach the body.

Slocum had thought Jacqueline might have returned to the grave site, but the infrequent imprints of her shoes showed she had not approached the cairn. She had passed within ten yards but had not stopped. Slocum looked ahead and up to the rim of the mesa.

"She went up there," Slocum said suddenly. He had no evidence for saying this. It simply seemed right.

"There? That's a steep climb, even if we find a path," Chettum said.

"You might get back to the stage in time to ride on into Hard Rock," Slocum said, taking a long drink from the desert bag. It was starting to get hot, and he was sweating profusely.

"I'll tag along," Chettum said. Slocum offered the man some water, watching closely as he drank. Nothing made much sense from the time he had boarded the stage in Laramie. Jacqueline knew Chettum somehow, and her departure had bothered the man more than he wanted to show. He was not willing to let Slocum hunt her on his own. The peddler had died of fright, and all the driver wanted was to get to Hard Rock so he could go on a bender.

Of all the improbables, that one made the most sense to Slocum. He wouldn't mind tying one on right now, either, especially if the Digging Fool's proprietress was as pretty as Old Gus claimed. Instead, he skirted the base of the mesa hunting for a path to the top.

A scuffled area alerted him that his hunt was at an end. Slocum could not be sure but thought he recognized the outline of Jacqueline's small shoe. She had come unerringly to a path up the side of the mesa. This made Slocum wonder even more if the driver didn't have the right idea. Get drunk, forget all this.

He started up the trail, not bothering to look back to see if Chettum followed.

"Wait, Slocum, don't go," the man called. "You want to take the water bag?"

Slocum turned to take the water bag and saw Chettum going for his six-shooter. Slocum hurriedly looked around and saw nothing for the man to shoot at—other than John Slocum.

The first bullet missed Slocum by inches. It went singing off toward the top of the mesa. Chettum fumbled with his six-gun, struggling to cock it again. Slocum's hand flashed to his holster and gripped his Colt Navy. As quick as he was, he had forgotten he stood on a pebble-strewn path. The quick draw threw him off balance and sent him reeling. When his boot heel slid from under him, Slocum sat down hard. This gave Chettum time to fire a second time, but this shot was no better aimed than his first.

"What are you doing?" Slocum shouted. "Why are you trying to kill me?"

The ricochet from the second shot faded fast, drowned out by a rumbling that shook the ground. Slocum flopped flat on his back and craned his neck to look up the trail. A half dozen large rocks had come loose from the wall of the mesa and tumbled down toward him.

Rolling fast, Slocum avoided a third shot and lay face-down in a rocky trench with his arms up to protect his head. The first of the avalanche hit him and knocked Slocum senseless. Then the rocks pelted him and hammered at his flesh until he was groggy. Long minutes after the last rock had rolled downhill, Slocum lay stunned.

Slowly, painfully, he pushed away rocks that had tried to put him into a premature grave. Slocum shook himself and knocked off a layer of dust, then remembered what had caused the rock slide. His hand shot to his six-shooter, then he relaxed. Clay Chettum was nowhere to be seen.

Slocum slipped and slid back down the trail to where

Chettum had tried to gun him down. The pile of rocks might have buried Chettum. Or the gunman might have hightailed it. Slocum didn't see hide nor hair of the man, either under the rocks or anywhere near.

"Chettum!" he called, hoping to flush the man so he could shoot him. Slocum was only mildly disappointed when he got no answer. Chettum must have been buried by the avalanche.

Slocum turned and looked back up the trail. Jacqueline had come this way. If he wanted answers, she was the only one likely to furnish them. Hitching up his gun belt, Slocum began the climb to the top of the mesa.

Sundown came as a relief. All day Slocum had hiked along the trail carved precariously in the side of the towering column of rock. Not once did he see a trace of Jacqueline Renard, nor did he expect it on such a path. Hard rock never took the imprint of a foot well, and there were only a few low bushes. None had caught a bit of the woman's dress to give him proof he was on the right path.

Slocum stumbled onto the level mesa top in time to see the sun balance on the far side and then slip down. It took less than ten minutes before the stifling heat of the day turned to chilly nighttime. Knowing he had only a short while before the twilight vanished entirely, Slocum hurriedly sought Jacqueline's tracks. He walked westward, using the pale light reflected off the ground to catch any small rise for spoor. He saw tiny clawed-foot tracks left by hopping kangaroo rats, some larger tracks leading into prairie dog towns, and even a silver dollar–sized footprint left by a coyote. No human tracks showed.

With prairie dogs popping up all around and chittering angrily at him, Slocum began searching in a large arc from the top of the path. By the time the stars came out, he knew he had to give up. If Jacqueline Renard had come this way, he'd missed her tracks.

Slocum was a good tracker. He might have missed her. More likely, she had not come to the top of the mesa, and he had been on a day-long wild-goose chase in the hot sun. Slocum wiped his dried, cracked lips and wished Chettum had not vanished so completely with the desert bag. He needed water. Bad.

Giving up his hunt for the woman, Slocum started looking for water and food to keep himself alive another day. The search yielded him a small pool of clear water hidden in a shallow rocky depression. Grateful for the water, Slocum dropped to his belly and shoved his head into the pool, drinking deeply. Only when he began to feel bloated did he back off and look around.

A slow smile came to his lips. This was an oasis for more than a solitary human. He saw rabbit tracks in the muddy bank around the pool, as well as the imprints from larger creatures. Killing a deer would give him a huge meal, but that would be wasteful. Slocum picked up a rock, found a spot in the shelter of a wall of stone and waited. Less than twenty minutes after he had sated his thirst a careless rabbit hopped up to do the same.

The rabbit died, and Slocum dined.

The fire he had cooked the rabbit over began to gutter and burn down after an hour or so, but Slocum was not inclined to hunt for more dried wood to build it back up. The top of the mesa was short on trees and other shrubs large enough to furnish much firewood. The wind began whipping along the mesa, chilling Slocum to the bone, but he was too tuckered out to spend any time hunting for a better campsite. He had the water in the pool and was sheltered a little by a wall of rock.

Slocum snuggled down in the soft dirt blown up against the stony wall and knew morning would come too soon, with its burning hot sun. As he drifted off to sleep, he wondered what had become of Jacqueline Renard.

Then his thoughts turned to other matters, such as why

the peddler had died. The man had death on his mind back in the stagecoach, but he had given up the ghost fast at the base of the mesa.

Ghost.

The thought fluttered across Slocum's mind, but he discarded it as ridiculous. He did not believe in such things. During the war he had walked battlefields and had seen only the dead and the dying, with no hint that any of his friends and comrades—or enemies—continued to haunt the blood-soaked land after death.

Then came the ear-splitting shriek that brought him upright, heart hammering. Slocum had never heard such a mournful cry, such a soulful wordless wail of utter desolation, from man or beast. The sound faded, and Slocum settled down. For an hour there was no other unusual noise. After that, he tried to ignore the new, even more disturbing sounds that persisted through the night.

3

Slocum stretched aching muscles, and rose to splash water on his face. He had slept poorly due to the peculiar cries all night long keeping him on edge, but something more troubled him. Worse, he could not put his finger on exactly what it was. After drinking his fill from the pool and wrapping his water-drenched bandanna around his neck, he set off for the edge of the mesa and the trail down.

Halfway to the rim, Slocum realized what bothered him. He stopped, turned quickly and looked behind him. Heat shimmers danced along the mesa as the sun rose and heated the rock. High above circled a lonely buzzard waiting for him to show signs of flagging. But amid the tumble of rocks and the low, sun-baked dunes he saw only small movement of animals hunting and being hunted before it got too hot.

The feeling he had identified was one of being prey. Someone—something—was hunting him.

Slocum rested his hand on the ebony handle of his six-shooter, looking for any hint of trouble. If Chettum had survived, he might be inclined to shoot Slocum in the back. But nothing moved on the mesa that shouldn't be there.

Slocum still had the sensation of eyes following his every move. He backed up a few paces, then took his hand off his six-gun. Fighting what could not be seen was enough to drive him as crazy as the peddler. Slocum spun, found the steep path leading down the side of the mesa and reached the base just after noon.

Resting until almost twilight, Slocum felt rejuvenated even as his mouth turned into gummy cotton. He wished Chettum had not had the water bag with him when the rocks crushed him. Slocum considered digging for the man's body, then discarded the idea as hopeless. So many tons of rock would also burst the desert bag. Whatever moisture it had held would long since have been sucked into the parched ground.

Slocum began hiking for the road, putting one foot in front of the other and not thinking about the distance into Hard Rock. The dying heat of day was soon replaced by a growing chilliness. Deserts went from one extreme to the other, neither being too hospitable to a man on foot.

About a mile down the rutted road across the alkali plain Slocum heard a familiar sound. He stopped and slowly scanned the horizon. The sun had set and his night vision was a little weak after enduring the brilliant day, but there was nothing wrong with his hearing. Slocum turned slowly until he homed in on the sound, then he whistled. Waiting a few seconds, he whistled again.

The pounding hooves set his heart beating a little faster. The horse that loped over a nearby rise came directly to him. It was lathered and had a wild look in its eyes, but it was obviously used to being around men. As it got closer, Slocum saw a bridle dangling from its mouth.

"There, old fellow," Slocum said, reaching down and scooping up a trailing bit of severed bridle. "Who'd you get away from?" He examined the leather and decided one of the stagecoach team had broken free from Old Gus. This wasn't a saddle-broken horse but was probably hungry and thirsty and wondering when anyone was going to tend it.

Slocum spent a few more minutes gentling the horse, then swung onto its back. The horse reared and tried to buck him off, then subsided when it realized he was sticking like a fly to flypaper. He turned the horse's head toward Hard Rock and began riding slowly, getting used to the feel of the horse and letting it grow accustomed to the unusual weight on its back. Not pushing it, Slocum camped around midnight. The horse was thirsty and hungry, but not nearly as much as Slocum.

He reached town just after dawn the next day to a peculiar reception. Slocum rode slowly down the main street of Hard Rock, aware of how everyone looked at him as if he had grown three heads. Still, the feeling of so many people watching him in silence was not as spooky as the feelings he had experienced on top of the mesa. These were living, breathing folks and probably wondered why he was riding bareback into their town.

Dismounting, Slocum wrapped the tattered bridle around the hitching post in front of the stagecoach office the best he could. The horse reared and tried to break free until Slocum patted it and soothed it.

"That there's one of our horses, mister," came a quavering observation. Slocum glanced over his shoulder to see a portly man with a walrus mustache looking fearfully at him. The man stood inside the door of the stagecoach office and looked like he would bolt if Slocum said "Boo!"

"Much obliged for its use, too," Slocum said. "I was on foot east of town and would have been another two or three days out there if it hadn't been for this fine animal." Slocum patted the horse again. "It's no saddle horse, but are you willing to sell it?"

"How'd you get outside town like that? On foot?" The

man asked the questions as if he suspected he already knew the answers.

"I went hunting for the woman passenger who vanished from your stage a couple days ago. Did the driver make it to town all right?"

The man swallowed hard. His head bobbed as if it was mounted on a spring.

"Why's everyone staring at me like this?" Slocum pointed to the men up and down the street poking their heads out like prairie dogs watching for danger. When he looked at them, they all ducked back inside.

"Gus said you was dead. You and all the other passengers."

"He's mostly right," Slocum allowed. "About the others, at least. I'm thirsty and hungry but otherwise intact."

"The two men and the woman," said the man Slocum now pegged as the station manager. "They're all dead? You're sure?"

"One's dead. Chettum and I buried him," Slocum said, remembering how the peddler had died so strangely. "But Chettum and Miss Renard . . ." Slocum's words trailed off.

"The other passengers?" pressed the station manager.

"I can't say about them. I think they're both dead, but I never saw their bodies," Slocum said honestly. He doubted Jacqueline Renard had ever reached the top of the mesa, in spite of his gut feeling that she had, and he had never seen Clay Chettum's body after the man had tried to backshoot him. The avalanche had obliterated any trace, one way or the other.

Slocum frowned, wondering where Jacqueline had gone—and why. If she had been lured away, who had done it? The way it had worked out, her disappearance had given Chettum the perfect opportunity to gun Slocum down. But why? They had not been the best of friends from the beginning, but Slocum saw no reason for Chettum to try to kill him the way he had. It was all a puzzle now lost out in the desert.

"You figure they got family we should notify?"

Slocum shrugged. He pointed out of town at the edge of the mesa barely visible from the middle of Hard Rock. "What's the name of yonder tabletop?" he asked.

"That's Ghost Mesa," the manager said uneasily. "Folks don't go there much. The place is haunted."

"Haunted?"

"Ghosts of Injuns and miners who went up there when the first strike was made here in Hard Rock. The miners quick as a flash abandoned their hunt there, and a good thing, too. We got the richest danged mines in all Wyoming up in the hills."

He indicated the mountains festooned with tailings and dark burrows going into the rock. Slocum had been in enough towns to recognize the symptoms of rot. Hard Rock stunk with that decay. The easy silver had been pulled from the hills and what remained was declining in both quantity and quality. Only no one in Hard Rock was willing to admit it. The stagecoach station manager would be out of a job when the last mine closed. The merchants would no longer sell equipment and supplies if the miners moved on to richer, newer claims somewhere else. The tension Slocum felt in the town was that of waiting for the other shoe to drop.

"What do I call you?" asked Slocum.

"What? Me?" The man played with his mustache as if it comforted him. "Oh. The name's Underhill. Roy Underhill."

"Pleased to make your acquaintance," Slocum said, happy to be able to make anyone's acquaintance after his trek through the desert—and on Ghost Mesa. "What do you want for the horse?" Slocum asked again.

"That nag? Why do you want it? It's trained to pull a stage, and we need all the horses we can get. Not main out here, if you hadn't noticed, mister." Underhill seemed mighty defensive. Slocum thought he still had not accommodated himself to losing three passengers, then finding the fourth had survived.

Or maybe the station manager was trying to weasel out a few extra dollars for the horse. If so, Slocum decided it wasn't worth the effort haggling.

"Any reward for returning it?" Slocum asked, changing his tactics. This startled the portly man. "For all that, you willing to refund my ticket since I walked most of the way?"

"Most?" sputtered the manager. "Why, you only walked ten miles or so. That's only a small fraction of the trip, and you did use our horse for part of the trip. Might get you a refund of ten percent, and you'd be danged lucky for that much."

"What about Miss Renard and Chettum? And the peddler?"

"They'll have to claim any refund in person. Can't go 'round just handing out money, no sir." Underhill swallowed hard and stepped back into the office, as if he feared Slocum might come after him. Slocum's attention was fixed on a small saloon that might just have some food along with a bottle of whiskey.

"I'll be back to collect the money after I wet my whistle."

"You goin' to the Digging Fool?" asked the manager.

"If that's the name of the saloon," Slocum said. What had been a sign on the front of the two-story building had probably been ripped off in a high wind or by a particularly drunk and reckless patron, and never replaced. Slocum went on instinct that the nondescript, signless building was the single place in Hard Rock he wanted the most right now.

"I'll get the paperwork done and see how much I can refund," Underhill said, swallowing hard again when Slocum turned toward him and rested his hand on the worn butt of his six-shooter. "No need to get testy, mister."

"Slocum, John Slocum. My name's on the passenger list."

"Yes, sir, Mr. Slocum. I'll do what I can."

"See that it's enough to cover my bill." Slocum was tired of talking to Underhill, and headed for the Digging Fool Saloon. He had gone half the distance when he saw a man walking purposefully toward him. Somehow, it did not surprise Slocum too much when he saw the battered star on the man's vest glinting in the morning sun.

"Wait a second," the marshal called, hurrying up to Slocum. They stopped in the middle of the street. "I got questions to ask you."

"I was going to hunt you up when I got something to drink and put some food into my belly," Slocum said. His stomach growled to emphasize his hunger.

"What happened out on the road? Gus was mighty vague about it all."

Slocum detailed how the peddler had died and all that had happened afterward.

"Don't sound like you know much," the marshal said, stubbled jaw jutting out belligerently. Slocum saw the lawman didn't like him.

"Any part of my story that doesn't ring true, Marshal," Slocum said, "can be checked on. Just hike up to the top of the mesa and you'll see where I spent the night."

"Mesa?"

"The stage manager, Underhill, said it was called Ghost Mesa." Slocum's eyes widened when the marshal took a frightened step back. The lawman's eyes went wide and his mouth opened and then snapped shut. He turned and almost ran to get away without saying another word.

"Should have mentioned Ghost Mesa earlier," Slocum muttered to himself. He went to the Digging Fool Saloon and rattled the doorknob. It was mighty early for a drinking emporium to be open, especially if the miners had flocked to town the night before. The last of them might have been turned out only hours earlier. The owner, the barkeep and anyone else working in the saloon were probably asleep, trying to get enough shut-eye to cater to the miners again tonight.

As Slocum feared, the door was locked. As he turned to find any other place to eat in town, he heard a key in the lock. The door opened and showed him a glimpse of heaven.

Standing in the door was about the loveliest woman he had ever seen. She was tall and willowy, with small breasts the size of apples that pressed firmly and delightfully against the crisp white blouse she wore. A gingham skirt swirled from her trim waist. She pushed back a strand of nut-brown hair from her eyes and frowned at him.

"Sorry to disturb you, ma'am," Slocum said. "I need to get some food and thought the saloon might be open."

"Food? You're not looking for booze?" She eyed him from head to toe and back, her ginger-colored eyes boldly fixed on his.

"Water would do me better than whiskey right now," Slocum said. "I just got in from being stranded out in the desert for the last couple days."

"Were you on the stage that Old Gus abandoned? You were one of the passengers?" The shock in her voice took Slocum aback.

"Yes, ma'am. I had to bury one passenger and went looking for another who wandered off. Reckon I didn't do much of a job finding her since I lost the other passenger along the way."

"Out by Ghost Mesa?" The way the woman spoke told Slocum everyone in town was in awe—or fear—of the mesa where he had spent the night.

"It is."

"I . . . come in, please. I can rustle up something for you to eat. It won't be much."

"Ma'am, anything would be fine with me right now. My stomach's rubbing up against my backbone."

"The name's Starr Halliburton. Call me Starr."

He introduced himself, then followed her into the empty saloon, enjoying the view from the rear as much as he had from the front. Starr Halliburton was one fine-looking woman.

"You run this place?" Slocum asked.

"How'd you know? Oh, what a silly question," she said, smiling. "There's no reason for me to be here alone this early in the morning, otherwise."

"Something like that," Slocum said. His mouth watered when she put a plate of roast beef, day-old bread and a large beer glass filled with water on the table in front of him. "This is a feast."

"After being stranded by Old Gus out in the desert, I can well imagine." She pulled up a chair and sat opposite him, watching as he ate. Slocum was a little self-conscious but his hunger and thirst were too overwhelming for him to be bothered. When he finished and pushed back, he felt worlds better.

"That was exactly what I needed," Slocum said. "How much do I owe you?"

"You went after the other passengers? You tried to find them? Why?"

"The desert's no place to be wandering around aimlessly. It is mighty dangerous out there."

"Yes, Ghost Mesa," Starr said, nodding. She fixed her ginger eyes on him and looked as if she had come to a decision. "You were up there. Can you go again?"

"Why would I want to do that?" asked Slocum, intrigued.

"It might be that's where Peter and the others ended

up. Or perhaps they were just killed and their bodies left for the buzzards."

"Peter?"

"Almost a month ago, Peter and three others left on the stage for Laramie. They never arrived and the stage company has no idea what happened. Peter and the others are still missing, as well as the stagecoach, team and the driver."

"Road agents?"

"Over the years, there have been several gangs working that stretch of the county," Starr said. "Right now there seems to be only one, but it makes up for the rest with sheer viciousness. Peter might have been killed by road agents—or maybe something else happened."

"What else might that be?" asked Slocum, intrigued in spite of himself. He had no reason to hunt for her boy-friend or the other passengers, even if a reward went with finding them. Hard Rock wasn't the sort of place he intended to spend any more time than necessary, and he was only passing through on his way to somewhere farther west.

Anywhere farther west.

"There are strange tales told about the mesa. Some of them might be true. I can't imagine why Peter would go up there, or why the stagecoach would even slow down as it went past, but no one has spotted any trace of them along the road in a month, and that's the only other place they might be."

Slocum remembered the peculiar wraithlike fog that had wrapped around the peddler before he died of fright. There were many things Slocum could not explain in the world, some he cared not to examine too closely, but this one puzzled him. Had the same thing happened to Starr's friend Peter?

"You'll do it?" she asked eagerly.

"No, I won't," Slocum said firmly.

"The look on your face. What—"

"Never mind. I was thinking about something else." He spoke curtly but deep down he was curious. That had got him into trouble many times over, but not this time. Still, the peddler had died, and where had Jacqueline Renard gone? Something on top of Ghost Mesa was out of the ordinary. He had felt it every second he had walked along its rocky expanse.

"I'll pay you," Starr said, chewing at her lower lip. "It won't be much, but I can pay you to find Peter."

"Why me?"

"No one else in Hard Rock is willing to leave his mine or—" Starr bit off the rest of her sentence, then said, "There's no one in town willing to help. You have the look of a man able to do a chore like this."

"What look is that?" Slocum asked, amused. His green eyes locked on Starr's ginger eyes. He felt himself stirring, aroused by her beauty, excited by the nearness of a woman so determined. Slocum felt a long leg moving against his under the table, sexily, arousingly.

"You have the look of a man who gets what he puts his mind to," Starr said, moving around the table. She took his hand, placed it over her left breast and pulled it down firmly. Slocum felt the firm apple-sized breast under the crisp white cloth and the way the nipple capping it hardened with lust.

"You seem to be a woman who gets what she puts her mind to also," Slocum said.

"Yes." Starr moved sinuously like a hunting cougar and sat on his lap. Her lips parted slightly, then fixed on his in a potent kiss that sent Slocum's heart racing. Starr kissed passionately, then her tongue snaked out and lightly teased the tip of his tongue. Their mouths moved restlessly as Starr crushed her body into his.

"I'm getting mighty uncomfortable," Slocum said, breaking off the kiss.

"I imagine you are," Starr said, slipping off his lap and kneeling in front of him. Her nimble fingers worked on his gun belt, then quickly unbuttoned his fly. His manhood came leaping out, as eager as a racehorse ready to run.

She dipped down, her ruby-red lips engulfing him. Slocum groaned in pleasure when the lovely woman's mouth began moving all over him. When she added her dancing tongue to the stimulation, Slocum's hips lifted a little off the chair. He laced his fingers through her long, clean brunette hair. Slocum began guiding her head in a rhythm that excited him most.

When he thought he was not going to be able to stand it even an instant longer, the woman pulled back and looked up at him. Lust was etched on every line of her beautiful face.

"I want more," Starr said simply. She stood slowly and stepped back. Slocum watched as she unbuttoned each button on her blouse, revealing the snowy white mounds of her breasts little by little. With a sudden rush, she threw back her blouse and stood naked to the waist.

"That's about the prettiest sight I've seen in a long time," Slocum said.

"And this is about as long as I've seen in a spell," Starr said, reaching down and stroking up and down his fleshy shaft. New tremors of desire jolted Slocum at her touch. He reached for her, but she danced away, spinning so her skirt rose up and revealed her bare feet and bare legs—and even higher.

She stopped turning, then unfastened her billowing skirt. She stepped lithely from it, completely naked. Slocum's gaze fixed on the nut-brown thatch between her slender legs, then worked up her body taking in the breasts, the curve of her throat, her lips, her lust-filled eyes.

Slocum shucked off his shirt, stood and got out of his pants.

Wordlessly, she flowed into his arms. Slocum held her close, relishing the feel of her heat, her body, her passion. They kissed hard again. Starr's slender leg rose and circled Slocum's waist, pulling her crotch in hard against his. He reached down and cupped her rounded buttocks, lifted and held her suspended around his waist. This pressed her nether lips into his manhood.

Walking forward two steps, Slocum perched the woman on the edge of the table. Starr lay back then, her legs still around him and keeping him close.

"Go on," she urged. She reached down and took him again, guiding him into her most intimate recess. Both of them gasped when he sank balls deep into her tightness. Starr stretched back, arms high above her head, and arched her back. This crammed her down even more firmly into Slocum's crotch.

Slocum bent over and licked and kissed at her nipples, slipped down the slopes of her breasts then worked up to her swanlike throat. Starr took his face in her hands and kissed him with unbridled need. He returned the kiss in kind. Then he began moving his hips. A little bit to start but with firmer strokes, more determination, more desire. She was clinging hot and tight around his hidden length. This sent arrows of desire into his loins and drove him on.

With her legs locked behind his back, he wasn't going too far—even if he had been so foolish to want that. Starr tensed every time he lunged forward, her legs adding to the power of his stroke. They worked together well and their emotions built quickly. The heat of the woman's body and the friction of his shaft within her lit the fuse to the powder keg deep inside.

He grunted and began moving faster. Every stroke was

potent and lifted Starr's rump off the table. She twisted and turned and held onto him fiercely.

"I'm close, John, so close, so—ohhh!"

She crushed him flat when she climaxed. Slocum thought she would break him off at the balls. Her fevered response set him off. His hips flew wildly, and he buried himself as far into her body as he could with every thrust. The fuse sizzled and burned and finally reached the powder keg dangling between his legs. He arched his back and tried to ram himself entirely into her yearning tunnel. Slocum gasped as he spilled his seed.

Sweating, tired and spent, he stepped away. Starr's long legs dropped on either side of his body and dangled off the table. She propped herself up on one elbow and looked at him with those intense ginger-colored eyes.

"It's been a while since I enjoyed anything that much," she said.

"You won't hear me arguing," Slocum said, relishing the look of the naked woman sprawled on the tabletop.

"Will you?" she asked.

"What? Find out what happened to Peter and the others?" Slocum thought for a moment, then came to a decision. He wasn't heading anywhere in particular. What did it matter if he hung around Hard Rock for a few more days to help Starr? He had some questions of his own that he wanted answers for.

"Yes," Starr said.

"I'll find your friend," Slocum said.

Starr blinked and then laughed.

"What's so funny?" he asked.

"I thought I'd told you. Peter's not my friend. He's my husband."

4

Slocum stewed as he left the Digging Fool Saloon. He felt he had been used, but he wasn't going to go back on his word. It never did anyone any good fooling around with another man's wife, even if she was as pretty as Starr Halliburton. Even worse, he was supposed to find the woman's husband after having made love to her. Common sense dictated that Slocum find a horse, mount up and ride like all the demons of hell were nipping on his heels.

If they weren't now, they would be if he found Peter Halliburton alive. Slocum doubted any man was forgiving enough to thank a man sleeping with his wife for rescuing him. It got even more complicated if Halliburton were dead, as he likely was. If no one had found him in almost a month, the road agents had left him dead out somewhere out in the desert.

Or on Ghost Mesa.

Starr had to know this was a chance, and in a strange way, Slocum hoped it was the way it turned out. That way he wouldn't be making love to a married woman. Even that passing thought made him feel bad because it meant she was a widow.

"Damnation," he snorted, kicking at a rock in the middle of Hard Rock's main street. He had been roped and corralled before he had known it.

The best place to start his hunt was the stagecoach office. He poked his head in, startling the plump manager so much that the man's mustache twitched uncontrollably.

"I don't have authorization to pay you anything, yet, Mr. Slocum," said Underhill, obviously wishing Slocum would fade away like a desert mirage. "I'll let you know when I do."

"Maybe you can answer a couple questions for me," Slocum said, entering the office and pulling up a chair to sit across the desk so he could watch the manager carefully. Everything made the station manager more nervous, for no good reason.

"Doubt it. I don't know anything. Nothing at all, no, sir!"

"You lost a stagecoach to road agents about a month back. All the passengers, the driver, the coach and the team. Just disappeared without a trace."

"Well, yes," Underhill said reluctantly. Slocum felt as if he were pulling teeth rather than asking questions.

"Any trace since then? Anyone shooting off his mouth in town? Has Old Gus spotted wreckage that might belong to the stagecoach along the road?"

"No, nothing, nothing," the man stammered. "Th-there's a reward. Five hundred dollars."

Slocum let out a low whistle. That was a respectable reward. Then he frowned.

"No takers? Not even the marshal?"

"Marshal Dunlap's a fool, but not that big of one," Underhill said.

"So anyone out to collect is a fool?" Slocum leaned back in the chair, tented his fingers under his chin and stared at the man's bushy mustache, hypnotized by the way it quivered even faster. The topic of the lost stagecoach bothered him more than it should, even if he had the onus put on him for losing the whole kit and caboodle. Slocum saw that the manager's star was probably setting for a variety of reasons, not the least of which was the most recent loss by Old Gus of all his passengers, except Slocum.

"I wouldn't say that, but the road agents are a nasty bunch."

"Is there one gang or several working the route?"

"Why—I—what difference does it make? Dead's dead, and they'd as soon kill you as look at you. I have to make special plans every time I ship silver to Laramie."

"There wasn't any silver on the stage with Peter Halliburton?"

"No." The manager's flat statement came without hesitation, and Slocum was inclined to believe him. Trying to sneak a shipment past aggressive outlaws was a fool's errand, but he needed more information before he rode out hunting for Starr's husband.

"Where might be the best place to hijack a stage?" Slocum asked.

"You fixin' to go into business yourself?" The man's eyes darted to the worn butt of Slocum's six-shooter, then left to move everywhere but to return Slocum's direct gaze.

"I can't find them if I don't know where to start. You think Marshal Dunlap has an opinion on this?"

"He never leaves town, except to serve process and to bury the occasional body out in boot hill."

"A busy man," Slocum said, heaving out of the chair. "Give me the horse and you can keep any rebate on my ticket."

"What? Why, well, all right. That's more 'n fair, I suppose."

Slocum left, shaking his head. He now owned a horse that barely tolerated a rider, having been trained to pull a stage with a team, but he thought it was a good deal. He might wait until he died of old age for approval of any refund.

Walking around town, Slocum spoke with a few of the tradesmen and got a feel for how things worked in Hard Rock. The marshal kept a loose rein on the miners, and that suited everyone. He did not tolerate murder, but that was about it. No one Slocum talked to had ever heard Dunlap even broach the possibility of forming a posse and stopping the road agents. More than this, Slocum found the townspeople were not overly inclined to talk about Peter Halliburton or his wife.

That struck him as odd, since small towns, even boom-towns, thrived on gossip. Such a lovely woman, and the town's only saloon owner, losing her husband ought to have sparked all manner of discussion. If anything, it stop-pered it up tight.

Slocum went to the livery where he found Old Gus sitting with a younger man, swapping lies and sharing a bottle of whiskey.

"Heard you'd made it back alive. Danged if I know how. Can't imagine why you'd run off like that to find anyone, even a filly as purty as that one back in the coach with you. You find her?" Gus tilted his head to one side and fought to focus his eyes. He failed.

"Still looking," Slocum said. "I reckon there's no rea-son I shouldn't widen my hunt and see where Peter Hal-liburton went, too. There's a big reward for the information about that lost coach."

"My best friend got kilt on that stage," Old Gus said. "I'd known Inky fer well nigh two months. He was a newspaper fellow over in Laramie and got fired, so he come out here. Mining wasn't for him but drivin' was. Had quite a talent for it."

"How do you know that Inky is dead?" asked Slocum. "Did you see the body?"

"Don't have to. Anybody vanished for more 'n a day or two out there's sure to be dead."

"He might have made it to the top of Ghost Mesa," Slocum said. "There's plenty of water up there. Game, too."

"Wouldn't know 'bout that. That place scares the hell outta me." Old Gus took a long pull on the whiskey and choked. "Never catch me goin' up there with all them haunts floatin' around, either."

"Why hasn't anyone organized a posse to go after the road agents?" asked Slocum. "Looks like easy money to me, with such a big reward offered by the stage company."

"Not if them varmints are hidin' out on Ghost Mesa," Old Gus said. "I'll risk my neck drivin' past 'em. No way am I ridin' into sure death chasin' 'em up onto the mesa."

Slocum frowned and didn't understand the problem.

"If the ghosts don't do anything to the road agents, why should the ghosts bother you?"

"Maybe they got an accommodation with the ghosts," suggested Gus's drinking partner. "Sell their souls to them Injun ghosts in return for a safe place to hide. Who knows how them redskins' spirits think?"

"Yeah, who knows," said Slocum, seeing he was at the end of this line. "I need my horse tended to. Curried, fed and watered." He jerked his thumb in the direction of the skittish horse that had carried him to the safety of Hard Rock.

"That's the sorriest nag of my team. You shoulda held out for somethin' better, Slocum," Old Gus opined. "Still, the reason the mare was no good was that she'd been a saddle horse 'fore the company hitched her to a team."

Slocum nodded. The horse had obeyed simple commands, telling him it was not a complete loss trying to ride her.

"I'll see to her, mister," the liveryman said, coming

from inside the stables. "Soon as I help them finish this." He tapped the almost-empty bottle Gus and his friend had passed back and forth.

A loud crash drew Slocum but not Gus or the stableman. Three boys picked up rocks and threw them at something out of his sight. As Slocum rounded the corner of the stable, he saw five men already hard at work chinking stones at a man cowering by the Digging Fool Saloon.

"What's going on?" he asked a tow-headed boy.

He got a dirty look as an answer until the boy threw another stone that hit its target squarely.

"Left my slingshot at home or I'd really get 'im," the boy boasted.

The victim for the men and boys' ire cowered away, then lit out dragging one leg slightly, forcing him into a gait not quite a shuffle but not a run, either.

"Paiute?" asked Slocum.

"Of course it is," the boy said, sneering. "Can't keep them red-skinned thieves outta Hard Rock, no matter how we try." The boy shouted and ran after the retreating Indian. Slocum watched, knowing the boy had heard his father or someone older speak those identical words. The best he could tell the Paiute had wanted nothing more than to go to the general store down the street from the saloon.

At an impasse in Hard Rock, Slocum decided to move his search for Peter Halliburton farther afield. He went back into the livery and saw that the stable hand still worked at the bottle. Slocum saddled his horse, taking care to be gentle and move slowly around her. In time the horse would be used to his ways, and he would learn the mare's. Right now he didn't want to end up getting bucked off, maybe breaking a leg and being stranded. He had escaped the desert once. Surviving the waterless heat twice meant pushing his luck to the limit.

Slocum was glad his quarry was unable to move very fast because his horse decided it was time to make a bid for freedom. The mare bucked and jerked around, forcing Slocum to take a few minutes to gain mastery. By the time he rode along the road out of Hard Rock, the Paiute was out of sight.

The Indian might have gone to ground, thinking to avoid the stoning that way, but Slocum doubted it. Too many men and boys would be hunting for any trace of an easy target. The smart thing to do was leave Hard Rock entirely and return to wherever home might be.

The Paiute had headed in the direction of Ghost Mesa, but Slocum doubted any Indians lived on the mesa. That was sacred ground for them, not camping grounds in spite of what the stableman had said. The road agents might have their hideout on top of the mesa, but they needed a bigger trail to get up and down. The only path Slocum had seen was the small footpath he had taken to the top while searching for Jacqueline Renard. It had been unsuitable for anything wider than a man's shoulders or perhaps a surefooted mule. Still, the mesa was a large one and a dozen ways to the summit might exist that he had not seen. All Slocum had explored was the face toward the road.

Outside town, Slocum began riding in ever-widening arcs, hunting for the trail left by the Paiute refugee from town. It took the better part of an hour for him to find the proper tracks. The man's left foot turned out, forcing him to drag it slightly. Slocum doubted two men with the same deformity would have come this way recently. From the sharpness of the tracks, he figured the Paiute had come by less than a half-hour ahead of him.

Slocum rode slowly, keeping the sporadic trail in view as it curled away from the main road and went to the south of Ghost Mesa. Picking up the pace, Slocum tried to overtake the Indian. To his surprise, he never spotted his quarry by the time he reached the tumbled-rock region at the bottom of the soaring mesa. Slocum dismounted and looked around for new tracks, but the Paiute had vanished. On terrain like this, a herd of cattle wouldn't leave prints.

Slocum pushed back his hat, scratched his head and looked up at the mesa.

"Why couldn't you have gone to the northern side?" he grumbled. The hot sun cast deep shadows all over the rock face, giving hundreds of hiding places for anyone knowing the lay of the land. As he scanned the rocky side he spotted what had to be another trail leading up.

Slocum walked to the foot of the path. Like the other one, this was barely wide enough for a man to walk. Unlike the other, this one showed signs of recent use. An eagle feather had become wedged between two rocks. Slocum pried it loose gently and examined it. Glue made from deer hooves clung to the base, indicating the feather had fallen from an Indian's headdress.

A few feet farther along the path, Slocum found a bright yellow bead and then a tiny bit of silver. The path was well-traveled by these indications, but not on horseback. Reluctantly leaving his mare at the bottom after taking as long a drink of water from his canteen as he could, Slocum began trudging up the trail to the top of the mesa.

The heat beat down on him, but he grimly kept moving. This was no time to rest. He kept a sharp eye out for sign of the Paiute on the trail ahead of him but saw nothing. The Indian might have chosen a different route or even have skirted Ghost Mesa entirely. How he had so cleverly eluded Slocum told of fear—or long practice. The way the boys in Hard Rock acted rippled all the way up to their elders.

It was past two in the afternoon by the time Slocum stumbled over the rim and onto the level top of the mesa. Some distance, maybe a mile or more to his right, lay the pool of water he had discovered on his first trip here. His canteen was empty and his mouth was a desert in its own right, but he ignored the need for water right now because of what he saw in the other direction.

Ten minutes hiking brought him to a rocky field where dozens of graves had been opened. The stench turned Slocum's stomach and forced him to pull up his bandanna to cover his nose. He advanced cautiously and peered into the nearest grave.

"Well, don't that beat all," he muttered.

The fresh corpse had been stripped naked and everything that had been in the grave with the brave was missing. The Paiutes buried jewelry, knives, bow and arrows, pots and other items the deceased might need in the Happy Hunting Ground. All of it was gone.

Stolen.

Slocum went from grave to grave. Each was in the same condition as the first. The smell died down a mite as he went farther toward the center of the mesa. These bodies were desiccated, the flesh strung across the skeletons like old, dried-out leather. Slocum wasn't sure if he did not prefer the fresher, more odorous corpses. These were a mockery of life. A life stripped of all belongings.

Grave robbers, Slocum decided. He put his hand on his six-shooter and scanned the horizon. In most places he could see the edge of the mesa, but as he turned toward the north the rugged land blocked his view. An entire Indian village could be hidden in the middle of the mesa and he would never know it.

He began spiralling out around the graves, trying to determine what was taken. Mounds of broken pots and shards from other pottery told him the robbers sought only valuable items like silver and turquoise jewelry. Slocum stopped and poked through one robbed grave and shook his head. That wasn't quite right.

Clothing and weapons were missing, also. Such would be of value only to another Indian, and he could never see that happening. The Indians were terrified of ghost sickness, becoming infected with the roaming spirit of the departed. They would never willingly disturb any of their own graves.

Even if the Paiutes were at war with another tribe, Slocum doubted their most bitter enemy would desecrate a graveyard. The looting had been done by white men. He was as sure of it as he could be of anything.

He cut through the burial ground, heading for the path back down the side of the mesa. Slocum had learned nothing of value and had only dug up more questions he could not answer. How any of this grave robbing tied in with Peter Halliburton's disappearance was beyond him to figure.

Before he reached the newest of the graves, Slocum slowed. Every sense came alert. The hot, still afternoon air carried only the smallest of hints to him of the attack.

He whipped out his six-gun and threw himself to one side in the same movement. Slocum hit the ground hard, rolled and came up in a grave, sharing it with the newly dead. A bullet sang past his head and took off his hat. Ducking instinctively, Slocum waited a second, then poked his head up again for a quick look.

Three Paiute warriors made their way across the burial ground in his direction. Two carried rifles and the third held a bow with an arrow nocked and ready to fly.

Slocum knew how it had to look to them. He had been wandering around in their most sacred ground. The graves had been robbed, and he was the one most likely to have done it. Even if they had watched him from the instant he had climbed to the top of Ghost Mesa, they wouldn't be too inclined to listen to anything he had to say. Someone systematically looted the graves, and the Paiutes had no way of knowing Slocum wasn't scouting out new sites to plunder.

He feinted, as if he intended to make a run for the path

down the face of the mesa, then went in the other direction. The Indians would likely have let him run to the path because he would have been a sitting duck all the way to the desert floor. Slocum stumbled and flopped belly-down in another grave in time to avoid two rifle shots that kicked up stone and dust in his face.

Rolling onto his back in the grave, feeling the corpse poking into his side, Slocum fired and fired again at the Paiute rearing up behind him. The brave's arrow launched and missed Slocum's chest by a fraction of an inch; Slocum's bullet found its target. The Paiute clutched at his chest as a red flower blossomed on his bare skin, then he sank down to join his comrades in death.

Slocum regretted killing the man, but it was his life or the Paiute's. He had no quarrel with them, but they obviously did with him—or with other white men pilfering their graves.

Another quick peek over the edge of the grave got Slocum a faceful of dirt as a slug narrowly missed him. He got off a quick shot and heard the grunt of pain. It wasn't a killing shot, but he had winged his foe. Taking a deep breath and steeling his resolve, Slocum did the only thing he could do.

The odds were as good as they were going to get. He surged up over the side of the grave and charged. His sudden, unexpected attack took the Paiutes by surprise. The unwounded one's next shot went wide. Slocum's ended the warrior's life.

Then Slocum tumbled to the ground as he wrestled with the warrior he had wounded. The Indian was strong and was slippery from both sweat and blood, but Slocum was uninjured. The wound weakened the Paiute and allowed Slocum to wear him down.

They rolled over and over until Slocum came out on top. He looked down into a face showing nothing but utter hatred. He cocked back his fist and let fly. His knuckles crushed into the Paiute's chin, and the brave went limp.

Panting, Slocum got off the man and considered cutting his throat. It didn't pay leaving an unconscious enemy behind, especially when he would be exposed on his way back down the path. Slocum spat blood. He had cut his lip in the fight and never noticed it until this moment. The scent of death around him and the coppery taste of blood in his mouth decided him.

There had been too much needless killing.

He used his thick-bladed knife to cut strips of rawhide from one of the dead Indian's deer-hide pants and used the strands to bind the one he had knocked out. Slocum stared at his handiwork and decided it would take a spell to work free.

Long enough for him to get the hell off Ghost Mesa.

5

The ride back to Hard Rock seemed longer than the ride out. Slocum ached from bruises and cuts sustained during the Indians' attack, and the horse under him had to be watched constantly. For some reason, it had become jumpier. Looking back over his shoulder at Ghost Mesa, Slocum wondered if that was the reason.

Did the horse sense something he did not? Slocum had learned to rely on the senses of horses and dogs and other creatures in the wild. They were even more finely tuned to trouble than his own senses were.

It was well past sundown when he reached the edge of town. Slocum knew immediately this was a boomtown from the way the Digging Fool Saloon was packed to overflowing with customers. More than one drunk miner stumbled outside to fall in the street where scavengers swooped down to rob the poor fools of any money still in their pockets. He frowned at such open lawlessness. Marshal Dunlap ran a wide-open town.

The livery stable held only a lone horse. Slocum guessed Old Gus had taken his team and driven the stage out onto the road to Laramie again. How he had missed the stagecoach on the road was beyond him, but he had spent a considerable amount of time hiking up and down the side of Ghost Mesa—and fighting the Paiutes there.

Slocum tended his horse, currying the mare, feeling her and being sure she had enough water before he left to go to the saloon. Piano music from inside was loud and off-key, but no one complained. From the way the miners crowded the bar and downed the whiskey, they weren't in the mood to complain about anything. They were too intent on getting soused.

It came as no surprise that Starr had a flock of men around her. Slocum watched the lovely brunette for a few minutes, seeing how she fended off amorous advances and still sold more whiskey to her would-be paramours. At that thought, a cold lump formed in Slocum's belly. Starr Halliburton was married, and he had made love to her on the very table where she sat with a half dozen miners. Slocum's sense of honor was strict about such things; common sense also dictated this was the way to trouble.

But she was so lovely. Starr threw back her head and laughed, making her amusement at the bawdy joke seem genuine, although Slocum suspected she had heard it a hundred times before.

"Mr. Slocum!" she called, seeing him. The woman motioned him over. "Have a drink."

"He a friend of yers?" growled one miner missing two front teeth and sporting more scars on his lined face than any two other men in the saloon.

"He is, Clete. A very good friend." The ginger-colored eyes fixed on Slocum and danced with merriment—and something more? That made Slocum a mite uncomfortable. She saw nothing wrong in cheating on her husband with him. What would Peter Halliburton say about it, if he strutted into the room at this very instant?

"Wall, then, lemme buy the varmint a drink. Sit here, Slocum, and lemme pop the cork on a new bottle of this here tarantula juice. Best damn rotgut in all Hard Rock."

"It's the *only* place you'll get whiskey in Hard Rock, Clete," Starr said, grinning.

As she told the miner of her monopoly, this set Slocum to thinking along other lines. Why was the Digging Fool not in the middle of a dozen other saloons? A town this size usually ran one saloon for every fifty or hundred miners. The hills around Hard Rock were filled with operating silver mines. Even if half were abandoned that meant upward of five hundred miners toiled to pry loose silver from a chary earth. He should see at least ten saloons in town, not one.

And not one run by such a pretty woman.

"You watch after her, hear?" Clete fixed a bloodshot eye on Slocum before he got to wobbly legs and staggered to the bar. The others around the table quietly drifted away when it became obvious Starr wanted to speak to Slocum alone.

"You've got a devoted following," Slocum said, noting how the miners honored the woman's privacy.

"It's hard-won, believe me," she said, smiling. Then her smile faded. "Did you find out anything about Peter?"

Slocum took a deep breath before answering. This was still a sore point with him.

"I did a bit of scouting but couldn't find where the stagecoach went," he said. "Finding the road agents might not be too easy, so I thought I'd ask the only other folks out there what they had seen. I trailed a Paiute from town."

"That must be Limp Foot," she said. "He's about the only one of them who comes into town."

"From the reception he got, I can see why."

"The miners aren't too tolerant when it comes to Indians," Starr said, no apology in her voice. "You think Limp Foot might know something about Peter?"

"I doubt much goes on around town that the Paiutes don't see. Tell me about them."

Starr shrugged. The simple movement caused her breasts to rise and fall, sending a lightning bolt of memory through Slocum. He remembered what those compact, shapely breasts were like without a cloth sheath around them. He forced himself to think only about finding her husband.

"When silver was discovered in the hills above Hard Rock, the Paiutes complained about all the prospectors poking around."

"Around Ghost Mesa?"

"The prospectors learned to avoid it, but they're a superstitious lot."

"You don't believe the mesa is haunted? Old Gus does. So does the man at the livery stable."

Starr laughed lightly and shook her head. "They believe anything they see through the bottom of a whiskey bottle. The big veins of silver weren't found out on the mesa, so there's been no reason to go out there. Do you think Peter's out by Ghost Mesa?"

"I trailed Limp Foot and lost him. I poked around the mesa but didn't see anything showing your husband had been there within the last month or two."

"What happened?" Starr fixed him with her brown eyes. "What did you find?"

"Nothing having to do with your husband or road agents," Slocum said, skirting the question. For some reason, he didn't want to admit to her he had fought with the Paiutes, even if he had bested them and lived to brag about it. He felt a little dirty at having poked around in the opened graves, although he was not one of the grave robbers.

"What aren't you telling me?"

"Is anyone selling Indian jewelry around town?"

"I don't think so," Starr said, taken aback by what seemed to her an abrupt change in the conversation. "I've heard some miners fancy Paiute feathers. Some wear silver bracelets or rings, but I don't know any by name, and most of the miners come through the Digging Fool sooner or later."

"Who might be selling the Indians knives or other weapons?"

"They make their own knives," Starr said, frowning. "John, what's going on? What did you find?"

"It's nothing," Slocum said.

"I've heard the Paiutes are getting mighty upset over grave robbers. I haven't seen anything definite but it sounds as if you stumbled onto something."

"I don't see how it ties in with your husband's disappearance, but it might," Slocum said. The pieces of the puzzle were all jagged and jumbled but deep down he felt that everything fit together—if only he could find the right order.

"But it might?" Starr sounded more excited now and her cheeks showed a light flush. "I took a silver bracelet in trade for a bar tab a few days back. Do you want to look at it?"

"Was it Paiute design?"

"I wouldn't know, but it could well be. It had bits of turquoise mounted on it, and I took a fancy to it."

"Who gave it to you?"

"Don't stare, John, but he's seated at the table at the far side of the room. A really tough customer. He makes me uneasy, but I've dealt with harder cases."

Slocum shifted his chair slightly and looked in the direction Starr indicated. The man in question sat with his back to the wall so no one could come up behind him. He played poker in what appeared to be a careless fashion unless one or more of the men in the game with him were in cahoots. Then they worked to fleece the two miners who had no idea about odds or cheating.

"He's doing a good job of cleaning out the pokes of those miners," Slocum observed. The man raked in a pot and looked both left and right, unconsciously identifying his partners.

"Clete," Starr called as the drunken miner returned with a bottle already a quarter drained. Slocum was glad it wasn't farther to the bar. Otherwise, the miner would never have returned with even a single drop of the amber fluid in the bottle.

"Whut kin I do, lovely lady?"

"Do you know that gentleman's name? The one playing with Sam and Danny Boy?"

"Ain't no gennelmun," Clete slurred drunkenly. "Shootist, 'less I miss my guess. Name's Gunnison."

Slocum left without a word, to Clete's delight. The miner got the woman all to himself again. As he made his way across the crowded room, Slocum shifted enough to be sure the leather thong on the hammer of his Colt Navy was pulled free. He wanted to be ready for anything.

He stared at Gunnison as the man deftly dealt the cards around the table. Glittering on the man's brawny left arm was a silver bracelet studded with various colored stones.

"Whatya starin' at?" demanded Gunnison, noticing Slocum's interest.

"Never seen a man wear a bracelet before."

"Took it off a dead Injun," Gunnison said. "A trophy, since I don't take scalps. You want to make something of it?"

"I'd rather play cards," Slocum said, glancing at the men around the table. Gunnison and his two friends bilked the miner directly in front of Slocum. The miner took his cue, pushed back from the table and silently indicated that Slocum could take his place.

Seating himself, Slocum wondered what he had gotten himself into. There was no reason to play poker with these men. He already knew they were cheats and, as Clete had observed, Gunnison had the hard-bitten look of a gun-slinger about him. That, more than anything else, made him stand out in the Digging Fool Saloon. Slocum had not learned anything by scouting for the missing stage-coach and Starr Halliburton's husband, so he had to try something else.

If anyone he had met in Hard Rock was likely to know anything about the road agents, it was the man across the table from him.

Every move caused the silver bracelet on Gunnison's wrist to sparkle, distracting Slocum a mite. That might be why Gunnison wore it, but Slocum doubted it. The man's vanity was immense. This was evidence of how he had gotten the better of a Paiute—or as Gunnison had said, taken it off a dead Indian.

One already in his grave.

"Haven't seen you around town before," Gunnison said, dealing carefully. Slocum saw how the man dealt seconds, giving a precisely chosen hand to everyone at the table.

"Haven't seen you around either," Slocum said, looking at his cards. Gunnison was willing to let him win a hand or two before trying to win it all back, and more, with a single big pot.

Slocum's answer rocked Gunnison back. The gun-fighter stared at him for a moment, then laughed harshly.

"You got quite a mouth, don't you?"

"I've got quite a hand," Slocum said, seeing he had been given three queens. "Ten dollars."

The betting went quickly, and Slocum pulled in a pot worth almost a hundred dollars. The next pot Slocum also won. When he saw how Gunnison straightened in his chair, he knew this was supposed to be the hand he lost all his money.

Before Gunnison could deal, Slocum pushed back from the table and announced, "I got a powerful thirst, gents. Cash me out."

Gunnison's eyes went wide in surprise.

"You're winnin'. You can't leave when you're ahead. Not after just two hands."

"Can and will, since you're dealing from the bottom of the deck. That is, when you're not dealing the second card in the deck to your friends."

"You callin' me a card cheat?"

Silence fell in the saloon and miners began clearing a path directly behind Slocum, in case the lead flew and missed his body.

Slocum saw how Gunnison's two confederates also moved away from the table so they could get to their six-shooters. He had intended to rile up Gunnison so he could find out more, but he had gone too far.

"Gentlemen, please, have a drink. Champagne. On the house!" piped up Starr Halliburton. She pushed between Slocum and Gunnison, holding a half-filled bottle out as a peace offering. Slocum saw by the look in Gunnison's eyes he wasn't going for the liquor. He wanted blood.

Slocum put his arm around Starr's trim waist and guided her to one side.

"This grave robber's just leaving," Slocum said. He saw his jibe hit home. Gunnison glanced at his wrist where the bracelet gleamed, then back at Slocum.

"This isn't over, mister," Gunnison said. He jerked his head toward the door, silently ordering his men out. The three left, glancing back to be sure Slocum didn't try to shoot them in the back. When the three had left, a collective sigh was released that sounded like steam being released from a freight train boiler.

"You live dangerously, John," Starr said softly. "That might be why I like you so much. Come on up to my room. It's on the second floor at the rear."

"Got business to tend to," Slocum said, knowing what it would lead to if he accepted the brunette's invitation. More than that, he wanted to see where Gunnison had run. He had flushed his quarry. Now he had to track him to his lair.

"You can't just shoot them," she protested. "Marshal Dunlap might not be the best lawman, but he draws the line at murder." The brunette looked apprehensive for his safety.

"I want to see where they go. That's all," Slocum assured her.

"Then you'll be back?" The hopeful tone in her voice weakened his resolve to the point he almost let Gunnison and his cronies go on their way. Almost.

"Count on it," he said. The merriment in the Digging Fool had returned, and he slipped through the crush of the crowd, popping out into the cold night air in time to see three men riding out of town.

They headed in the direction of Ghost Mesa. Somehow, Slocum wasn't too surprised. He hurried to the stables, saddled his protesting mare and followed at a distance, not wanting Gunnison to spot him.

A crescent moon turned the ground to silver, but this did not help Slocum track the three riders. He spotted the looming, dark mass of Ghost Mesa and headed for it, cutting directly across the desert. The mare turned skittish, not trusting herself to walk without breaking a leg in the numerous prairie dog towns scattered across the land.

Slocum fought to keep the horse moving. By the time he reached Ghost Mesa, he had to admit he had lost Gunnison and his men. They might not have even headed this way, but he had a gut feeling that they had. The bracelet Gunnison wore had been stolen from a Paiute grave atop the mesa, and the gunman had the look of a road agent about him.

He had no reason to believe it, but Slocum thought Gunnison might hold the answer to a lot of the crimes around Hard Rock. Including Peter Halliburton's disappearance.

Slocum rode around slowly, occasionally stopping to listen for hoofbeats. The usual desert night sounds were all he heard. Disgusted that he had lost the men, Slocum turned his horse back toward Hard Rock when he heard the soft, low moan. He reined in and looked back over his shoulder at the shadowy face of Ghost Mesa.

Lacy white clouds drifted from the rocky crevices, floated about as if caught on some unseen, unfelt wind, then vanished. Quick on the ghostly heels came the eerie, unearthly wails that he had first heard the night he had spent with the broken down stagecoach—the night Jacqueline Renard had vanished.

And the peddler had been driven mad enough to die of fright.

6

Slocum made his way up the rickety back stairs to the second floor of the Digging Fool Saloon. He tried the knob on the door, twisting it gently. Unlocked. He slipped in. The narrow hall to his right led downstairs to the noise and chaos of a room filled with drunken miners. Two steps to his left was a door—where Starr had invited him to go earlier.

This door was locked but a little jiggling caused the heavy door to bounce around enough for him to get it open without a key. Slocum ducked inside the room, then closed the door quickly to avoid being seen. His nose wrinkled at a curious odor in the room. Sulfur. It was faint and not what he had expected in Starr's room.

He lit a kerosene lamp and looked around the neat room. The bed had been made, the wedding ring–quilted bedspread neatly smoothed over it. Two fluffy feather pillows looked mighty inviting, but Slocum turned from them toward the wardrobe. He opened the door and again caught the strong sulfur odor.

From what he could tell, it came from Starr's riding clothes. While curious, it meant nothing. Slocum continued his illicit search of her room, not sure what he might find.

Opening the drawer in the bedstand revealed a small collection of rings and other trinkets. None was worth a bucket of warm spit. He closed the drawer and continued his search. After fifteen minutes, Slocum had to admit he had found nothing suspicious. Starr was everything she appeared to be—and said she was.

He felt guilty about searching her room, but he had to know for sure what he was getting himself into. A photo of her with a handsome man stood on the bedside table. Slocum figured this was her husband, but all other trace of the man had been removed from the room.

Slocum worked his way back through the door, taking longer to close it than he had to open it. When he finished, it was still locked. He doubted he had left any sign he had searched the room. Slocum started for the stairs when he saw a second room a couple paces down the hallway. This door was unlocked.

Poking his head inside, Slocum saw a more spartan room. In the wardrobe hung a few men's shirts and a pair of tattered pants. The bed sagged and looked as if it had been made hurriedly. A writing desk in one corner held enough papers to show this was Peter Halliburton's room. Slocum ducked back into the hallway when he heard the boards in the stairs creaking ominously.

"John!" cried Starr when she reached the top of the flight. "How'd you—oh, you came up the back stairs. Did you just come up?"

"Just did," he lied. The lovely woman took his arm and steered him toward her room.

"What's in there?" he asked, pointing to the room he had just searched. Slocum watched Starr's expression carefully and was not disappointed. Her face fell, then turned into a poker expression.

"That's Peter's room. We . . . we did not share the same room often. Often enough. This is my room." She fished for a key on a purple grosgrain ribbon around her neck and worked at the locked door. It failed to open. She kicked it in frustration.

"Let me try," Slocum said, taking the key from her hand. Their fingers brushed fleetingly. A thrill of excitement shot through him. Slocum vowed to be more careful dealing with Starr. He had to remember she was a married woman, even if her husband was probably dead. Until he could tell for sure, Slocum had to treat her with respect due another man's wife.

He inserted the key, jiggled it a bit then turned. The lock snapped open, but getting the door open proved even more of a chore. When he had left, he probably had broken a hinge.

"The whole place is falling apart," Starr said with a deep sigh, never suspecting he had been the one who had damaged the door. She sat on the bed and held her hands in her lap, looking disconsolate. The brunette looked up. The silvery moonlight slanting through the window caught her hair and turned it into something exotic while bathing her face in deep shadows.

"What did you find out, John? Is Gunnison responsible for the stagecoach robbery?"

What she meant was entirely different. Starr cared less about the stage robberies than she did about her husband. He read it in the set of her shoulders, even if her face remained hidden to him. Slocum almost went to the kerosene lamp and lit it but held back. He would have had to brush past the woman.

"I lost him and the two owlhoots riding with him out near Ghost Mesa," he admitted. "Gunnison has the look of a road agent about him. Would it do any good to tell Marshal Dunlap about him?"

"I doubt it. The marshal isn't too inclined to take it on himself to protect the stage. There's some dispute about payment between him and the stagecoach company."

"What's wrong?" Slocum asked. She seemed to answer

his questions, but he caught the undercurrent of dread in everything she said.

"I'm going to lose the saloon if you don't find Peter soon," she said, beginning to sob a little now. She dabbed at her eyes. "I'm such a silly goose, crying like this. But I don't want to lose the Digging Fool, not that it's mine exactly."

"Your husband owns it," Slocum said flatly. Women couldn't own real estate, even in a progressive territory like Wyoming.

"I feel so awful, John. I love Peter. I do! But he was never interested in running the Digging Fool, and I am. If he isn't found soon to sign some papers from the owner in Laramie, we'll lose the saloon."

"You're confusing me. What's this about the owner in Laramie? You said Peter was the owner."

"Well, he is. I run the place, but he had to borrow money to open the saloon. We couldn't find a bank willing to make a loan, so he borrowed it from a man named Jackson Johnson there."

"So if you don't pay off the note, this Johnson will foreclose? Maybe you could write him or even go to Laramie and talk with him."

Slocum saw there was more Starr wasn't telling him. He held his piece until she finally told him.

"I need the loan papers and deed to the saloon. Peter had them when he went to Laramie. He went to Laramie often on other business, and he never confided in me the details of his dealings."

"You could wait until Johnson shows up to foreclose, then deal with him," suggested Slocum. The intricately winding path of Starr's finances was beyond him.

"Th-that's why Peter was going to Laramie, to talk to him about paying off our note. He had all our money with him. Every time the stage comes in, I'm afraid there'll be a court order foreclosing on the Digging Fool."

"How much money do you have tied up in this place?"

"No," Starr said firmly, her jaw set and her head shaking from side to side. "I see what you're hinting at. I will *not* simply turn around and walk away. This is *my* business, and I will keep it going, no matter what!"

"But you don't have the money to pay off the loan?"

"I told you!" she cried, distraught. "Peter had *all* our money with him. I'm broke, John. We weren't well off before he disappeared, but without him, I'm both heartbroken and bankrupt." Starr heaved a deep sigh and added, "You know the law. I can run the business, but I can't own it."

Slocum stared at her for a few seconds, then said, "I'll do what I can to find your husband. I promise."

She looked up expectantly, but he was already heading out the door. He had gotten himself mixed up in a tar pot this time. The only way Slocum could see to get away from Starr and her problems was to find her husband.

And he wasn't likely to find Peter Halliburton alive.

The road agents were the most likely culprits in Peter Halliburton's disappearance. Slocum didn't know how to flush them out because he couldn't find where they were holed up. Try as he might crisscrossing the desert, he could not find any trace of them. Adding to his frustration, he saw no sign that Jacqueline Renard had come this way either. She had vanished as surely as a ghost everyone in Hard Rock claimed to populate the top of the mesa.

Slocum swung the reins around a low branch of a post oak and settled under the dubious shade to wait. He had tried and failed to find the bandits. That meant he had to change his tactics. If he couldn't go to them, they had to come to him. Settling down less than a hundred yards from the road, he leaned back, tipped his wide-brimmed hat down over his eyes and drifted off to sleep.

Slocum came awake in late afternoon when he felt the

ground begin to shiver under his back. He sat up, pushed his hat back and saw a dust cloud coming from the direction of Laramie. Another stagecoach rattled and clanked toward Hard Rock.

"Look sharp," he warned his mare. The horse snorted and shied away, not wanting him to climb into the saddle again. The day was hot and the water scarce.

Slocum watched as the stage crept toward him, but he paid less attention to the stagecoach than he did to the terrain around it. He had scouted the land enough to consider this the place where he would rob the stage, should the urge strike him. He had done his share of robbery in the past and knew how it was done but was not inclined to hold up the stage now. He had promised Starr he would find her husband.

Or her husband's grave.

He sat straighter in the saddle when he saw a small dust cloud down a ravine leading toward the road. This approach hid a rider until the stage route dropped down into an arroyo that had chewed its way across the road during spring runoffs. The driver had to slow or risk tipping over the stage in the sandy, steep area.

That made it perfect for robbers.

"Come on," Slocum urged, putting his heels into the mare's flanks. He didn't want to stop the robbery; he wanted to capitalize on it. It took more than fifteen minutes for him to circle and come on the road agents from the rear. When he reached the stage he saw Old Gus in the driver's box, looking dejected.

"You come to rob me, too? Yer too damn late," growled the driver.

"They head toward the mesa?" Slocum asked.

"You thinkin' on shootin' them owlhoots? Good! Shoot 'em in the belly and let 'em suffer!"

"I'll see you in town later. You can identify them when I turn them over to Marshal Dunlap."

"You got rocks in yer head, Slocum. There's three of them varmints. You got to get the drop on 'em or you'll be buzzard food." Old Gus jerked his thumb upward to indicate the single circling carrion eater waiting for something to die.

Slocum saw that the two passengers were all right. One had the look of a preacher and the other was a peddler. Slocum remembered how the last peddler on this route had died. He swallowed hard, looked in the direction of Ghost Mesa and knew he had a powerful lot to find out other than what had happened to Peter Halliburton.

The road agents' trail was easy to follow. Gus had said three men had robbed the stage, and their tracks bore this out. They rode along confidently, not trying to hide the hoofprints. Slocum slowed when he neared the towering spire of rock that dominated the countryside. The road agents had turned south and headed around Ghost Mesa along terrain Slocum had already scouted. He took full advantage of the rocky hills and ravines to get closer. Within ten minutes he heard loud laughter and men joking.

Slocum reined back. The trio had been too easy to follow, and he worried he was headed into a trap. He made sure his Colt Navy rode easy in its holster, then checked his Winchester. If he ended up in a fight, he wanted to be the one putting the most bullets into the air—and into his enemies.

Dismounting, Slocum advanced on foot, picking his way silently through the rocks until he found a rise overlooking a level area where the three road agents had camped. They had a small fire sputtering to life. The sun set and brought with it a cool breeze that caused Slocum to shiver a little. He stayed low on the hill, watching and waiting. The gang had more than three men in it.

Slocum expected to see Gunnison show up to claim his share of the booty. When that didn't happen within another hour, Slocum decided it was time to act on his own. Either Gunnison was busy somewhere else or Slocum had read the man wrong.

His sense of rightness was such that he knew Gunnison was as crooked as a dog's hind leg.

Slocum made sure his mare was securely tethered to a sturdy-rooted sagebrush, got his rifle and went hunting. He circled the road agents' camp, coming at them up a draw. The sides of the ravine were shoulder-high and gave him the opportunity to walk upright without being seen. He kept the three highwaymen in sight as he came up on where they had pitched camp.

"Been a good day, yes, sir, it has," boasted one. "We took down that there stage without a hitch."

"I thought the preacher man would shit his britches when you shoved your six-gun into his face," said another, laughing at the memory. "You told him to give you everything, and I reckon he did—and then some!"

The third man grunted and poked at the coals with a stick to keep the fire blazing.

"How much did you steal?" Slocum asked.

"You know how much. We got four or five hunnerd dollars worth of—" It took the first road agent that long to figure out neither of his partners had spoken. He went for his six-shooter and then froze when he saw that Slocum had the drop on him.

"That's real smart. You others drop your hardware," Slocum ordered. His Winchester roved restlessly from one outlaw to another. He thought he had them treed. He was wrong.

The quiet one at the fire went for his six-gun. Slocum saw the movement from the corner of his eye, went into a crouch, swiveled and fired in a smooth action. The robber's bullet went into the ground; Slocum's rifle bullet went into the man's chest.

The robber gasped, started to reach for the wound and

then realized he was dead. He slumped to the ground, the six-shooter falling from his nerveless fingers.

The other two robbers weren't inclined to shoot it out with Slocum, but they both turned into rabbits and high-tailed it. Slocum took careful aim and fired at one man. He stumbled, went to his knees and then flopped onto his back like a fish out of water.

"You shot me!" he shrieked. "You got me in the leg!"

Slocum ignored the robber and searched the dark countryside for the third robber. He listened, he sniffed the night air, he peered into every shadow but saw nothing of his elusive quarry. Disgusted at having to let one of the road agents go, Slocum went back to the camp and checked the man he had plugged in the chest.

He might have been playing 'possum, but he wasn't. Slocum had killed him with a single, well-placed shot. He turned his attention to the other robber, still moaning and whining about catching a slug in the leg.

"You don't shut up, I'll put you out of your misery for good," Slocum said, laying his rifle down away from the wounded man's reach. He whipped out his thick-bladed knife and slit open the man's tough canvas pant leg to expose the wound. It bled sluggishly but didn't threaten the man's life.

"Bind it up."

"What? You're not gonna help me?"

"Do it yourself. We're riding for Hard Rock right away."

"I can't!"

The man's whining annoyed Slocum. He turned and stared at the man. The robber saw tombstones in Slocum's eyes and hastily used a strip of his own pants to truss up the bullet wound.

"You want to ride or you want to walk?" Slocum asked. He had fetched the trio's horses and had already slung the dead robber bellydown over the back of one horse. Slocum worked to gather the loot and other gear that the three had strewn around the camp.

"Ride," the man said sullenly.

That suited Slocum just fine. It got them back to Hard Rock all the faster. He just hoped the man didn't try to escape—or talk. He was in no mood for conversation after losing the third robber to the enveloping night at the base of Ghost Mesa.

7

"Just take the money and vamoose," Slocum's prisoner said. "There ain't no need to put me in jail. I ain't got any reward on my head. We got danged near five hundred dollars there."

"I'm not interested in it," Slocum said, resigning himself to listening to the road agent try to wheedle his way out of jail for the next few miles into Hard Rock. "I might be interested if you'd tell me what happened to Peter Halliburton."

"Who's that? A friend of yours?"

Slocum heard slyness enter the robber's tone and knew anything more said would be a lie.

"Might be willin' to help you find him."

"Keep talking," Slocum said, using his spurs to keep the mare moving along at a steady clip. The horse lacked the stamina possessed by so many others he had ridden. He did not fault the animal, though. It had been trained to pull a stagecoach. It was a good life for a horse. All it needed to do was perform for a short while, perhaps only fifteen or twenty miles, then it stood in a corral or pasture for days more, unlike a saddle horse constantly on the trail.

"Well, now, lemme see. This friend of yours—what was his name?"

"Halliburton."

"Yeah, right, Halliburton. He's about my height, ain't he?"

Slocum rode in silence. He did not really know how tall Peter Halliburton was since Starr had not mentioned it. She had given a terse description of her husband, and Slocum had seen the picture in her bedroom but it gave no indication as to size.

"He is," the prisoner said firmly, getting into the swing of his lie. "We come across him a week or two back over in Laramie. He was livin' it up, he was. I can show you where."

"How was he living it up? In a saloon?"

"Sure, what other way is there? He had this red-haired whore. Never seen hair so fiery. She looked like she could turn a man into a pretzel and leave him beggin' for more."

"Halliburton," Slocum said. "What about him?"

"Him and this redheaded whore was whoopin' it up. But I ain't tellin' any more until you let me go."

"Last week?"

"Could have been. Might have been a little longer 'n that."

Slocum heard the lie in every word slipping from the outlaw's lips. The man was relating his own fantasies and not anything he had seen involving Peter Halliburton. Given the chance, every cent of the money stolen from the stage might have ended up buying the red-haired hooker's favors.

"I'll tell you anything you want, mister. Please give me the chance!" The pleading rose to a shrill whine now that they had reached the edge of Hard Rock. "I don't wanna go to jail! I never been in jail before."

"Get used to it," Slocum said coldly. He rode straight for the jailhouse, dismounted and dragged the man off his horse. Walking clumsily on his wounded leg, the road agent tried to elicit some sympathy with anyone who might see. It was early enough that only a few people in Hard Rock stirred.

Slocum banged on the jailhouse door until a sleepy marshal came to see what the commotion was.

"What you got, Slocum?" Dunlap demanded.

Slocum explained how he had come by his prisoner, about the man bellydown over the horse and how he had retrieved the loot stolen from Old Gus's stage.

"The station manager'll be real pleased to hear this. He's gettin' a lot of heat from the Laramie office over losin' so many passengers and so much money bein' shipped."

"They should put a shotgun guard on the stage," Slocum said.

"Not my business tellin' them what to do. You willin' to swear that this howlin' coyote is one of the robbers?"

"Gus can identify him, too," Slocum said. "They were too stupid to wear masks."

"That's not so!" cried the prisoner. "We had our bandannas on so's nobody could tell who we were. Not even that preacher fellow, even if he swore on a stack of Bibles." The man's voice turned into a tiny squeak when he realized how effectively Slocum had duped him into confessing his crime.

He turned sullen as the marshal shoved him toward the back of the calaboose. Slocum heard an iron door clank shut, sealing up one of his problems. But catching the robber did nothing to solve his other mysteries. What had happened to Peter Halliburton? And Jacqueline Renard?

"I'll hang onto the loot for evidence," the marshal said, eyeing the saddlebags filled with the money from the robbery. He licked his lips and Slocum could read the man's larceny as if it were an open book.

"And I'll go tell the station manager you're holding it

for him," Slocum said. "He'll be sure Old Gus is sober enough to identify the robber."

"They wore masks, didn't they?" the marshal said, jerking his thumb in the direction of the cells.

Slocum smiled slightly and left without saying another word. The marshal would figure it out eventually.

Stepping into the street caused a little stir. Men pointed at him now and whispered how he had brought in a prisoner and had another draped over the back of a horse. Slocum glanced in the direction of the still-closed Digging Fool Saloon and wondered if he ought to tell Starr what had happened. He decided against rousing her after what was probably another hectic night at work since he had nothing definite to tell her. When he found out what had happened to her husband would be soon enough to disturb her.

That's what he told himself, but he knew he was lying. He avoided her to keep from being drawn into her arms—and bed. Until he proved to his own satisfaction Peter was dead, Slocum wouldn't fool around with a married woman. For all he knew, the man locked up in the Hard Rock jail had told the truth about seeing Peter Halliburton over in Laramie with a soiled dove.

The only thing he could do was keep after the road agents and track down the ones responsible for the robberies and Halliburton's unfortunate disappearance. Slocum mounted, turned his mare's face back down the road and headed out for Ghost Mesa again. He had brought in two men. The third was out there somewhere waiting to be caught.

Slocum got off the ground, brushed the dust from his pants and hands then shook his head in frustration. The third man had vanished into the darkness as if it had swallowed him whole. The ground was rocky but held enough dirt here and there that ought to have given some sign.

Slocum had found nothing. No boot print, no fresh scratch on a rock from a spur, not even a broken limb or crushed leaf from the vegetation along the path he was certain the owlhoot had taken.

Ghost Mesa loomed like some malevolent hulking beast, towering upward and seeming to topple on him. Slocum involuntarily touched the butt of his Colt, then relaxed. It was only a mesa. He had seen hundreds like it in his day.

A tiny moan sent a thrill through him and caused Slocum to touch his gun butt again. Cursing himself as a superstitious fool, he went back to hunting for tracks.

The campfire left by the three road agents had long since burned itself out. Slocum used it as the center of a search that was as complete as he could make it in the dark. He considered waiting for dawn but worried the fleeing robber might put too much distance between them ever to be found.

He got his bearings after another fruitless search, saw the dim silhouette of a distant rock and set his course toward it. This was the direction taken by the running outlaw and, sooner or later, Slocum had to find some trace of the man. No one ran as scared as the robber had been without getting careless—or unlucky—somewhere.

More than this, Slocum thought it was about time his luck changed.

Trudging along stolidly, Slocum went directly for the spire of rock as the sun slowly came up. The chill night air hung on tenaciously, but the brilliant Wyoming sun eventually triumphed. Sweat began running into Slocum's eyes, forcing him to stop more often to wipe his forehead and get the burning salt from his eyes.

As he mopped his face, he looked down and saw a rowel in the dust. He quickly knotted the bandanna back around his neck and picked up the silver spiked wheel. It was slightly tarnished, but not as much as if it had been in the desert for a long time. The amount of discoloration was about what he'd expect to find on a careless man's equipment. He tucked it into his vest pocket and picked up the pace now. Although he walked, his mare began shying and neighing. When it bucked hard enough to jerk him around, Slocum finally took heed.

"What's spooking you?" he asked. The horse's eyes were wide with fear, and its nostrils flared.

Slocum froze for an instant, then released the reins and dived for cover. The horse had not been overly intent on the track as he had been. If he had paid more attention to the world around him and less to hunting for boot prints, he would have heard the slight scraping sound sooner. What galvanized him to dive for cover was the unmistakable sound of a six-shooter cocking.

The bullet whined past, well above his head, an instant later.

Slocum rolled onto his back, got his six-gun out then rolled again to find better cover. The ambusher was ahead along the trail and to the left. Slocum's keen eyes searched for any sign but saw nothing. During the war he had been a sniper, one of the best. He had thought nothing of lying flat on his belly all day in the hot sun, waiting for a Union officer's gold braid to glint and give him away.

This patience saved his life again. While he had been watching for the sniper ahead of him to give himself away, another had approached from the right. He caught the movement out of the corner of his eye, swiveled and fired in one smooth motion. He heard a gasp and knew he had winged his attacker.

Wounded, not killed. He faced at least two ambushers. One was wounded and still dangerous, and the other was unbloodied. Slocum knew there might be more, to boot. He cautiously shifted position, keeping the larger rocks between him and the trail he had followed. Moving forward, he came on the spot where the first sniper had lain. He saw how the gravel had been disturbed, how the toes of a pair of boots had dug into softer dirt, where the man's knees had been.

The sniper was gone.

Slocum chanced a quick look to the far side of the trail and spotted the crown of a Stetson. He got off a fast shot and cursed himself right away when it went sailing into the air. They were decoying him, forcing him to use up his ammo.

He moved even faster now, trying to get behind them. When he pressed his back against the rock spire he had used as a guide post, he turned back and waited. And waited and waited.

Slocum's patience gave out after almost fifteen minutes when he failed to hear as much as a gasp of pain or whispered instructions being passed between the ambushers. He knew he might be walking into another trap but had no choice. Standing in the hot sun all day would kill him as surely as a bullet.

Slocum worked his way back down the trail, this time on the side where he had wounded one gunman. He found specks of drying blood on a rock, verifying his accuracy. Not much farther away he spotted the Stetson with a bullet through the brim on the ground. Slocum strained to hear, to see, to sniff out his foes.

All he got was heat from the increasingly oppressive day. Insects buzzed, but not around a corpse. He caught small movement but only of small, harmless animals sneaking from their burrows to hunt food before the day got too hot. And all that expanded his nostrils was the usual desert smell.

Wary but seeing there was nothing he could do about it, he made his way back to where his mare stood uneasily. He gentled the frightened horse, then went toward the rock spire. His attackers had fired at him and then vanished into thin air.

It took him the better part of an hour to find how they had disappeared so quickly. Beyond the rock spire rose a sheer stone wall that masked yet another path up the side of the mesa. In dirt, on the mesa's rock face, just about everywhere, he saw where the two men had hightailed it up the path on foot.

To the top of Ghost Mesa.

Slocum reloaded his Colt Navy, then pulled the rifle from its saddle scabbard. Like the other trails up the mesa face, this was too small for a horse. Looking a few yards along the trail, Slocum saw places where the trail had collapsed, leaving yards or longer gaps that had to be jumped. For a man on foot, it was possible. For a horse, never.

"Be back before it gets dark," Slocum said, patting his horse. He slung his canteen over his shoulder after taking a healthy swig, wished he had water for the horse then started along the sloping trail.

Footsore and tired, he got to the mesa in early afternoon. The heat baked his head and made every step agony, but he kept going. No one tried to ambush him and lived to brag about it. More than the need for vengeance, Slocum wondered who the hell had been taking the potshots at him. He was certain the road agent had lit out on his own. Had he found a friend? Why hadn't they pursued the ambush more aggressively?

He had a passel of questions and had not found a single good answer. Yet.

Slocum took another drink from his canteen, then put it down at the head of the trail to free up his hands. He didn't want any distractions. He levered a round into the Winchester's chamber, then chanced a quick look across the mesa.

He cursed when he saw hoofprints. The two men had

either been met by others on horseback or had left their mounts here before going to the desert floor to ambush Slocum. Whatever the story, they had ridden off toward the middle of the mesa where a tumble of rocks provided an even better spot for ambushing him. A single sentry could keep watch on the entire tabletop. From the way the boulders were strewn around, it was a fortress that might be well nigh impregnable.

Slocum set out for it, keeping the tracks in view as he walked but always watching for any sign of movement ahead. He might not get as much warning this time as he had on the desert floor if he walked into another ambush.

When the hoofprints he followed split into two groups—one going north and the other south—Slocum saw that he had been trailing a band of at least five men from the trailhead. Three north, two south was the way he read the spoor. Two men had shot at him, so he went after the pair going to his right.

He had barely gone a dozen paces when the most soul-searing cry of agony he had ever heard in a life over-flowing with dying men rent the still, hot air. Slocum froze, his hand sweaty on the stock of his rifle. The sound might have come from some tortured animal. Slocum had the gut feeling it came from a man's throat.

He could not be certain but thought it came from ahead—the direction he was already walking. Common sense told him to get back to his mare and think about what all this meant in the safety of the Digging Fool Saloon. He had nothing to prove, and all that he was likely to find on the mesa was death.

Slocum's grip tightened on his Winchester as his stride lengthened. He had gone past curiosity. He wanted an end to this. He wanted to find Peter Halliburton, get a measure of revenge for the snipers shooting at him and then he wanted the hell away from Ghost Mesa.

Another shriek rent the afternoon. Slocum almost ran

in the direction of the scream. It was a plea for help as much as it was a death cry.

Slocum ran up a gravelly slope and looked down into a bowl-shaped depression on the mesa top. In the center of the sandy spit someone had driven crossed poles into the ground. Wrists savagely lashed to each of the uprights and legs dangling limply hung the road agent he had set out after.

Slocum didn't have to get any closer to know the man was dead. He had been strung up spread-eagle in the hot sun to die, and his last pleas for help had echoed across the mesa to lure Slocum on.

8

Tracking the five who had ridden away from the top of the trail to Ghost Mesa lost some of its appeal after Slocum saw the man crucified on the poles. He felt an obligation to get even with the pair who had shot at him, but not to the point where he ended up dangling by his wrists and becoming buzzard bait.

Slocum wasted no time retracing his footsteps down the broken path to where he had left his mare. The horse shied and tried to run, but Slocum gentled the horse enough to mount and ride back toward Hard Rock. The entire way he thought hard about what he was trying to do here. Starr Halliburton would lose the saloon to a financier in Laramie if he did not find her husband soon, but after so much time Slocum had to believe Peter was long dead.

Slocum had been shot at and vowed to repay that debt in blood, but not if it meant he would get killed trying. He suspected the crucified outlaw on the mesa was the man who had gotten away; he had been punished for losing the loot stolen from the stage. Dealing with road agents who thought like that sent a chill up his back. Moreover, Hard Rock held no appeal for him. It never had. He had boarded the stagecoach from Laramie only because it headed in the right direction. Slocum had no destination in mind when he had left Laramie, and he had none now.

"I promised," he said as he returned to town. Slocum knew he was on the hook until he either brought back Peter Halliburton's body or found the man alive, with a redheaded whore, drunk as a lord or simply living elsewhere to get away from Starr.

It was almost midnight and business was brisk in the Digging Fool Saloon. Slocum dismounted in front of the gin mill and again wondered why this was the only watering hole in town. It ought to make money by the bushel basket, letting Starr meet her bills and keep the Laramie creditors at bay.

"John!" Starr came running out, her cheeks flushed and her eyes wide. "What did you find? Any trace of Peter?"

Slocum looked around and saw a few miners sitting on the boardwalk in front of the saloon. They did not move but their heads turned, showing their interest in eavesdropping.

"Let's talk somewhere more private," Slocum said, taking Starr's arm. She pressed close to him as they went around the saloon to the back stairs. He remembered the feel of her body against his, her silky skin and wet kisses and passionate embrace. As much as Slocum wanted to push their lovemaking out of his mind, he could not. Starr was a very sexy woman.

Sexy and married—unless Slocum could prove otherwise.

Starr spun around and clung to Slocum. She began sobbing gently.

"I thought I'd lost you when you didn't come back."

"I haven't been gone that long," Slocum said.

"There were rumors. Two men came in and said they saw your body out in the desert."

Slocum went cold inside.

"Can you describe them?"

"I was busy in the back room and only heard when Leo—he is my barkeep—told me after they left," Starr said.

"Do you think Leo could describe them?" Slocum shook his head when he saw Starr's expression. Too many men came and went for the barkeep to single out two braggarts, even ones talking about dead bodies out in the desert.

There were too many questions and no answers. Had these men ridden directly into Hard Rock from Ghost Mesa? Why brag about ventilating Slocum unless the man and his partner were boasting to enhance their reputation among their gang? Or had they been told to spread the word to keep others from poking around trying to find Gunnison's hideout?

"Never mind. I keep finding bodies around and on Ghost Mesa, but none is your husband's. I can't even find the stagecoach he rode out of Hard Rock in."

"The man in the jail might know, John. He's my only hope."

"He doesn't know anything," Slocum said, more harshly than he intended.

"I have to try." The edge that came into Starr's voice told him argument was futile. She turned and flounced off, her skirts brushing the dirt and causing a small dust devil as she walked. Slocum watched and knew she was a fine, high-spirited woman, and one he could spend a pleasurable amount of time with.

He had promised to find her husband. Slocum told himself this over and over as he trailed her to Marshal Dunlap's bailiwick down the street. He slipped into the lawman's office as Starr finished making her plea to speak with the prisoner.

Dunlap glanced from Starr to Slocum and then back. He rubbed his eyes, showing he had been asleep.

"You bother him, you take the consequences," Dunlap said.

"What might those consequences be, Marshal?" asked Slocum.

The lawman grumbled something about letting sleeping dogs lie, then grabbed a key ring and opened the door leading to the cells in the rear of the hoosegow.

Dunlap looked sour as he jerked his thumb in the direction Starr had already taken. Slocum silently followed to keep the woman out of trouble. The road agent he had brought in was the only guest in the iron-bar hotel.

"Sir?" asked Starr in a tentative voice designed to give the wrong response from a prisoner. The man's eyelids flickered open and a lewd grin crossed his face.

"Well, well, the little lady's back to—"

"Shut your mouth," snapped Slocum. "She's got questions. You answer them truthfully and you might get to keep one or two of those teeth you still have."

Starr looked at Slocum in irritation, then turned back to the now frightened prisoner. Her fingers curled around the bars as she pulled herself closer.

"I'm begging you. Tell me what you can about my husband. Is he dead?"

"I—" The prisoner started to lie, but Slocum's presence put a cork in that bottle.

"How long have you ridden with Gunnison?" Slocum asked. He saw the man's expression and decided the matter in his mind: Gunnison was not the leader of this gang. Slocum drew back and let Starr ask her questions and get completely phony answers. The man wanted out of jail in the worst way and saw that Starr might spring him if he pleased her.

After a few minutes, Slocum took Starr's arm and gently pulled her from the cell door.

"But I was getting somewhere, John. He'll tell me what

he knows. I know he wants to cooperate but is leery of it. He fears I might double-cross him."

"He's a lying skunk," Slocum said, pushing Starr out of the jailhouse past Dunlap and into the cool night. The fresh air blowing off the desert wiped away the sweat on his forehead but did nothing to clear up his own concerns.

"Why do you say that? You thought he had something to do with Peter's disappearance. You—"

"I was wrong about him," Slocum said. Together they walked slowly toward the still-booming Digging Fool Saloon, stopping near the general store to talk. "I think Gunnison is responsible for your husband's death, but I can't prove it. From the look on that guy's face, he has no idea who Gunnison is."

"But he robbed the stage! He and his two friends. The ones you killed," she said, half accusingly. Slocum knew she wanted information and thought he had removed two good sources.

"I shot one. Gunnison or his gang did in the one up on Ghost Mesa for cutting in on their territory. But the three didn't know Gunnison. They were working on their own."

"That means they don't know what happened to my husband," she said in a weak voice.

"I'm afraid that's true," Slocum said. "It's the only thing that makes sense. There were two gangs out there robbing the stages. Two of this owlhoot's partners are dead—and he's left all alone." Slocum didn't go on to say that, had there been others in the gang, they would have tried to spring their partner by now. This jail was a cracker box and Dunlap was likely to simply open the doors without argument if anyone shoved a gun under his nose.

If another gang wanted exclusive rights to robbery along the road from Laramie, removing competition was logical. That explained the man crucified up on Ghost Mesa.

By Gunnison and his men? Slocum considered it likely.

"Why don't you think he knows anything, John? He said—"

"You're grasping at straws. He and his cronies never robbed a stagecoach in these parts before the one they stuck up the other day. He as much as admitted that, until it looked as if you might spring him if he told you what you wanted about Peter."

"I . . . I suppose you're right. I do want to find Peter." The brunette stared at the noisy saloon and heaved a deep sigh. Slocum found himself more intrigued by the rise and fall of her breasts than the problem confronting them. She was a mighty fine-looking woman.

He stared into shadows a few yards away cast by the general store. Something moved in the darkness, moving with soft *slip-slide* sounds. Whoever had been there had spied on everything he and Starr had said.

"Go on back and tend the crowd," Slocum said. "I've got something to do."

"What? Can you come back when the crowd's gone? Come to my room?" Starr smiled almost shyly, belying the racy costume she wore as proprietor of a saloon.

"We can talk more," Slocum said, anxious to get after the spy.

"I'd like that," she said, coming up on tiptoe to kiss him lightly. "Very much." With that, Starr turned and rushed off. Slocum licked his lips and tasted her wine sweetness all over again, then shook his head. It was safer crimping blasting caps in his teeth. Fooling around with a married woman was the most dangerous thing any man could do.

He slid the leather thong off the hammer of his Colt Navy, then headed down the alley next to the store. At the rear of the store, Slocum looked around for any sign of the man who had been eavesdropping. Going to one knee, he saw the footprints in the dirt and recognized them immediately.

Walking quickly, Slocum took out after the Paiute named Limp Foot. It took only a few minutes to find the Indian cowering behind the livery stable's water barrel.

"I'm not going to hurt you," Slocum said. "Come out so we can talk."

"You chase me before," Limp Foot accused.

"And you got away. You're a mighty fine trailsman." Slocum sank down, his back to the stable wall so he sat only a few feet from the Paiute. Limp Foot looked around nervously, then settled down, clutching a leather pouch to his chest.

"You no rob?"

"I'm not going to steal anything from you," Slocum said. "What do you have there?"

Reluctantly, Limp Foot opened the pouch and held up a silver necklace. Slocum recognized it as Paiute design, and one likely to have come from around the neck of a warrior buried atop Ghost Mesa. He figured he had found the grave robber.

As if Limp Foot read the thought in Slocum's head, the Paiute cried out, "I no steal from dead! They ride the Ghost Pony fast and get away real fast. To steal from them is not what I do!"

"They'd even the score after you died," Slocum said, wondering if this was the way the Paiutes thought of the afterlife.

"Warriors kill anybody stealing *now*," insisted Limp Foot.

Slocum held out his hand and waited for the Indian to put the necklace in it for his examination.

"Where'd you get this?" he asked, seeing it was most likely taken off a buried corpse, no matter what Limp Foot claimed.

"No steal, no steal!"

"Never said you did," Slocum said. "What else do you have? I might be interested in buying something."

"You?" Limp Foot looked skeptical.

Slocum shrugged and waited for the Indian to come to his own conclusions. The way Limp Foot had evaded him before told the man's skill out in the desert—and probably up on Ghost Mesa. Limp Foot must have lived in the region all his life and had learned every hidey-hole along with the rest of the Paiute braves. For all Slocum knew, Limp Foot might have been injured in battle rather than hobbling around from some birth defect in his foot.

"You like this?" Limp Foot pulled out a bracelet. One by one, the Paiute took out what he carried in his leather pouch, and one by one Slocum examined them. His interest was small until Limp Foot pulled out a pocket watch.

"Let me see that," Slocum said. The sharpness in his voice caused Limp Foot to recoil. If the Indian could have, he would have jumped to his feet and run off. "Sorry. I'm just interested in looking at it."

"You have watch. Why need another?"

"Show me what you have there," Slocum repeated more gently. This brought out the watch. Limp Foot dangled it from a gold chain, letting it swing slowly before passing it over.

Slocum caught his breath when he popped open the case and saw Starr's picture staring up at him. She looked as lovely in the photograph as she did in person. Turning the watch over, he saw the engraving: TO MY LOVING HUSBAND PETER. A small five-pointed star had been etched below the inscription.

"You like? Make good deal for it," Limp Foot said hopefully.

"As you said, I have a watch," Slocum said, knowing he had to dicker if he wanted more than the pocket watch. "But I can always use a spare."

They argued over the price. Slocum paid four dollars for the watch with Starr's picture in it. He wound the stem and studied it, holding it up to his ear to hear the steady ticking inside.

"Where'd you get this?" Slocum asked.

"No steal, no steal!" cried Limp Foot, again wary.

"You're too jumpy," Slocum said. "I like the watch. If you can get more like it, I'd buy them, too. Did you get it the same place you did the rest of this loot?" He pointed to the leather pouch with the rest of the Indian jewelry.

"No steal!" Limp Foot got to his feet.

"Just asking, that's all."

Slocum swung around when he heard gruff voices in front of the livery stable. The small distraction was enough to give Limp Foot the chance to fade into the dark, taking his stolen jewelry with him. Slocum started to go after the Paiute, then hesitated. What could he do to get the information he wanted from Limp Foot? Beat him? The Indian had come by Peter Halliburton's watch somehow, but honey drew more flies than vinegar. Slocum had to coax the information out of Limp Foot.

"Get them spare horses." The voice came from inside the stable. "The boss is gonna be ridin' in any time now."

Slocum pressed his face against the splintery plank and peered through a knothole in time to see a man leading four horses from the stable. Slocum pushed back from the wall and went around the side of the livery as each of the four men took the reins of the horses that had been in the stable and mounted.

"There he is now."

Slocum stepped out into the street, not caring if he was spotted now. At the far end of town rode Gunnison, but it was the man with him that startled Slocum the most.

Clay Chettum spoke to Gunnison with the easy familiarity of a partner long on the trail.

Slocum shook himself free of the surprise at seeing

Chettum not only alive but riding with Gunnison, and stepped into shadows. The four mounted men rode to where Gunnison and Chettum had reined back to greet the others. From his position, Slocum could not hear what was said. He hurried back behind the stable and went down two stores, squeezing between a narrowly separated bookstore and a bakery until he was less than a dozen paces from where the six men still spoke in their low voices.

"You boys ready?" asked Gunnison.

"All ready, boss. We got the wagon behind the store. Josey and Kirk are waitin' for us."

"Loot the damn place. Get every bit of food you can," Gunnison said. "Don't skimp on the rest, either."

With that, Chettum and Gunnison wheeled their horses and trotted from town. The other four rode in the direction of the general store and vanished behind it.

Slocum ran around, crossed the street and saw six men tearing a large hole in the rear wall of the store. Barely had the wood hit the ground than four crowded into the store and began tossing out bags of flour and beans, mining equipment and other supplies more fitting for an entire town than for a gang of highwaymen.

The marshal ought to be alerted, Slocum knew, but he had other fish to fry. He went back to the main street, past the general store being looted and grabbed the reins on his mare. The horse tried to rear, but Slocum kept his seat and got on the trail after Gunnison and Chettum.

He left town and was swallowed quickly by the blackness of the desert. The cool wind in his face energized him. Slocum tried to decide how startled he had been seeing Chettum with Gunnison and finally decided the answer was not as much as he might have been. After the landslide there had been no trace of the backshooting Clay

Chettum, and Slocum had wondered if the man might not have escaped.

He rode fast and soon caught sight of a pair of riders ahead along the curving road. Slocum slowed, then cut across the desert to overtake them. He was sure Gunnison knew more about Peter's disappearance than anyone else because he was sure Gunnison was the leader of the road agents preying on the stage company. If he had to get the details he wanted from Gunnison by going through Chettum, all the better.

Slocum had not forgotten how Clay Chettum had tried to shoot him in the back.

When he got back on the road, thinking he was in front of the two men, he was irritated to find they had disappeared. Slocum rode toward Hard Rock slowly until he found the arroyo the men had taken that cut across the road. It was dark, but the stars gave him enough light to follow their tracks. Neither Chettum nor Gunnison made any attempt to hide their path. And why should they? They didn't know anyone was after them.

The scent of burning wood came to Slocum's sensitive nose before he saw the snaky curl of smoke rising from a campfire. He dismounted and advanced on foot. Chettum and Gunnison had already tethered their horses to a nearby rope stretched between two scrubby cottonwoods. A single dark figure hunched over by the fire, poking at it and putting a coffeepot into the coals.

"Get me a cup of coffee," Gunnison ordered.

"Get the damned coffee yourself," came the answer. "I've been ridin' all day and I'm tired."

"Chettum," Gunnison said in a tone intended to send a thrill of dread down anyone's back. "Get it for me. Now. I got important things to talk over."

Clay Chettum hurried to the pot to pour his boss some coffee, but Slocum's eyes fixed on the trim figure rising to face Gunnison. The fire flared as Chettum poked around, sending out an orange glow that lit the woman's face.

Slocum thought he was past being surprised, but he was wrong. Jacqueline Renard took Gunnison into her arms and kissed him like she meant it.

9

Slocum edged around to get a better view. He drew his six-shooter, although he doubted he would need it as long as he stayed out of sight. Jacqueline Renard and Gunnison broke off their kiss and turned toward the fire, arms around each other. Chettum handed Gunnison a tin cup of coffee.

"You have everything on its way?" Jacqueline asked. Her tone was similar to the one she had used to order Clay Chettum around while they were passengers in the stagecoach.

The way Gunnison jumped told Slocum he was on the receiving end of Jacqueline's question.

"Kirk's got the wagon on its way now," Gunnison said. "He's a good man."

"I don't care about him. I want the supplies. I'm sick of living like a savage, eating nothing but hardtack, beans and rice."

"We'll be livin' high on the hog 'fore you know it, li'l darlin'. We got damned near enough money to paint San Francisco red."

"You don't have anywhere near enough," Jacqueline said coldly. "You know that's not what we agreed to do

91

until afterward. And don't call me 'little darling.' I find it offensive."

"You didn't object too much last night when we—"

Jacqueline punched Gunnison in the belly. Slocum involuntarily cringed when he saw how much force she put behind the short jab. Gunnison gasped and started to bend over. He fought to keep himself from showing any weakness in front of Chettum—and Jacqueline.

"There's the wagon," Chettum said, coming to his boss's rescue. "I can hear it."

"That's not a wagon," Gunnison said, swinging around. "It's a horse. A lone horse." He whipped out his six-shooter and waved it about wildly. Slocum ducked down and heard his mare raising enough of a ruckus to raise the dead up on Ghost Mesa. He wasn't sure what information he had learned about Starr Halliburton's lost husband, but he had definitely found out who was behind the robberies. With this information and the location of the camp, he might get the reward offered by the stagecoach company, even if Marshal Dunlap did nothing to arrest Gunnison and the others.

Slocum quietly made his way through the dark until he stepped into a hole and fell facedown. He landed hard enough to jolt his elbow and squeeze down on the Colt's trigger. The report from his six-gun echoed up and down the length of the arroyo, giving him away. Slocum scrambled to his feet, but his leg twisted under him again.

"There!" came Chettum's loud shout. "There's the son of a bitch who's spyin' on us!"

Sand all around Slocum kicked up as Clay Chettum started firing with more enthusiasm than accuracy. This prompted Slocum to stay low and scramble along on his hands and knees until he came to a bend in the arroyo. He got to his feet again, tested his leg and found it sound enough to run like a bat out of hell for his horse.

Slocum found out quickly what had spooked the mare.

Behind him pounded Gunnison and Chettum. From the direction of Hard Rock came the rattling, clanking wagon laden with stolen goods. To either side of the wagon trotted a pair of riders. Slocum was caught between the road agents on one side and their leader with his number one lieutenant on the other.

He swung into the saddle as one of the men in the driver's box spotted him.

"Hey, who's that? Get him! Shoot him down!"

Slocum got his horse galloping. He knew how dangerous this was in the middle of the night when the mare could not see the ground, but it was even riskier to stand and fight. With a little luck Slocum might have gotten the men on the wagon shooting at Chettum and Gunnison, but he couldn't count on that working—or working long enough to get away.

His best chance for survival lay in speed.

The mare's flanks heaved and lathered quickly from the exertion. Slocum kept the horse racing along at a full-out gallop until he felt the stride weakening and knew he would be walking unless he eased back. Turning his head to one side, Slocum listened for sounds of pursuit and heard nothing.

"Whoa, easy there, whoa," Slocum said, letting the horse slow and finally come to a halt. The mare stood on wobbly legs. Slocum dismounted to let the horse rest without his weight on her back.

Over the horse's harsh gasping for breath came the sound Slocum had missed a few seconds earlier. Pursuit. Gunnison had sent his gang after him.

Slocum knew running was out of the question now. His mare wouldn't make it a dozen yards before dying under him. He pulled his rifle from the saddle sheath and levered a round into the chamber. Slocum judged where the first rider would come over the bank of a ravine, aimed and waited. His finger drew back smoothly when the crown of a hat outlined itself against the darker horizon. By the time the rider's head was in Slocum's sights, his finger had pulled all the way back.

His Winchester bucked, and the rider flew out of the saddle. The fallen outlaw didn't make a sound, but the men behind him did. Slocum had sown the seeds of confusion in their rank. He jacked another round into the rifle chamber and waited.

But not for long. He got a second shot, but this one did not find the target he had aimed at. The slug caught the road agent's horse squarely in the chest and brought it down. Slocum wished he had hit the rider rather than the horse, but the dark cloaked his target and there was no way to take back his shot.

"Come on," he said to his mare. He mounted. The horse staggered slightly but did not balk when he gave the mare her head. Slocum fired twice more at what he thought were outlaws but knew right away he had wasted his ammunition. One slug whined off a rock, and the other sang harmlessly into the night.

Not pushing his horse gave it the chance to recover more. The road agents had lost their taste for his blood, but Slocum kept a sharp eye on his back all the way into Hard Rock. He dismounted in front of the hoosegow, every muscle in his body aching. Slocum brushed off trail dust and saw he had tangled with a thorn bush somewhere in the dark. Small cuts oozed and began to sting like insect bites. He ignored the pain and went into the marshal's office.

Dunlap jerked upright from where he had been sleeping on the cot at the side of the office.

"Damnation, Slocum, don't you *ever* let a man sleep?"

"I found the road agents' camp," Slocum said, dropping into the single chair in front of the marshal's desk. Dunlap grumbled and began pulling on his boots. While he dressed, Slocum took out the watch he had bought from Limp Foot and let it swing slowly.

Peter Halliburton's watch. But no sign of Halliburton.

"Where's this outlaw heaven?" asked Dunlap, pulling a tattered U.S. Army map from his top drawer. He spread it out for Slocum to point out the spot.

Slocum shook his head. He had no idea where the campsite was on the map.

"I can take you to it. They robbed the general store and—"

"What?" This caught the marshal's full attention. "Those sonsabitches!" he cried. Dunlap strapped on his gun belt. "I can't let 'em do that in town. Not when the silver's gonna be . . ." The marshal's words trailed off. "I shouldn't have said anything."

"You have a big silver shipment going out?"

"Just like the last one."

Slocum stared at Halliburton's watch, then at the marshal.

"The same stagecoach Peter Halliburton was on?" Nobody had mentioned a silver shipment before. Peter and the others probably had not known they were riding along on a surefire target for the road agents because Underhill had tried to sneak the silver out of Hard Rock to Laramie.

"Reckon so."

"What route was that coach supposed to take?" Slocum asked, looking more closely at the marshal's map. He saw a pencilled line meandering on seldom-used back roads before meeting the main route to Laramie.

"That's a secret," the marshal said sullenly.

"Because you're using the same route again?" Slocum shook his head. "Against this gang, you need a small army to guard the shipment. You can't sneak the silver past them."

"You sure they robbed the store?"

Slocum sank back, the hard chair cutting into his spine.

He was not going to get any cooperation from Marshal Dunlap. The man might be afraid of Gunnison and his gang.

"Gunnison is the leader," Slocum said. He started to mention Jacqueline Renard and then stopped. He wasn't sure why. Such an accusation might muddy the water, but Slocum felt the marshal was going to ignore his warnings anyway.

"You keep your mouth shut about that silver shipment, Slocum."

"When is it going out?"

"Day after tom—" Dunlap clamped his mouth shut, drew his six-shooter and rolled the cylinder to be sure the gun was loaded. Without another word, the lawman stalked out to verify a crime committed hours earlier.

Slocum left the jail, heaved a sigh and mounted again. The mare sagged under him.

"Sorry, old girl," he said, patting the horse's neck. "We have a bit more hunting to do. Then you'll get a bag of grain and all the water you want." He rode out of Hard Rock, this time following the route of the earlier silver shipment.

A lesser tracker would have missed it. Slocum rubbed his eyes to make sure his restless night at camp hadn't blurried them, then saw the way brush had been pulled out along the route. He hadn't found the tracks left by the missing stagecoach, and now Slocum knew why.

Gunnison's men had driven the stage off the back road, used the bushes they had pulled up by the roots to erase the tracks and then discarded the vegetation. The wind had long since blown away the shrubs, but where they had been uprooted showed plainly what had happened.

Slocum got off the path and soon found where the road agents had stopped covering their tracks.

"A little farther," he assured the horse, his eyes ahead

on the trail. The stagecoach had probably been driven to the stand of cottonwoods ahead and left there. No matter how thorough Dunlap had been trying to find this spot, he would have missed it unless he had a huge posse. From everything Slocum had seen of the miners in Hard Rock, that wasn't too likely. If anything, he thought the marshal had made a half-hearted attempt—by himself.

He dismounted, let the horse graze on the sparse grass around the tree trunks and went to the abandoned stage-coach. The team was long gone, probably taken by the highwaymen, but they had left behind a stage filled with bullet holes.

Slocum climbed into the driver's box and immediately saw the dark red stain on the hard wood seat. Some-body—the driver, Inky?—had bled a hell of a lot. Too much to still be alive. Slocum reached down and fished around for the strongbox. It was gone.

He jumped down and walked to the back. The tattered canvas flap over the boot had been ripped away. Deep cuts in the wood showed where heavy iron boxes had been dragged out and dropped to the ground. Slocum heaved a sigh. The silver shipment was long gone. Only then did he go to the passenger compartment. He dreaded what he might find there.

He wrenched open the balky door and looked inside. The compartment might never have carried passengers. Nothing had been left behind. Slocum slammed the door and looked around the stand of cottonwoods. From the way the trees grew, he thought there might be a small pool of water at the far end of the grove.

Halfway to his destination, Slocum found the strong-box. The lock had been broken and the contents dumped out. A scrap of paper caught under one edge of the heavy iron box was all that remained. But he was on the right course.

Slocum touched Peter Halliburton's watch in his

pocket, then walked on deliberately. Next to the small pond he had expected were four larger strongboxes. The Hard Rock silver shipment had been dug out of the boxes and transferred. Slocum carefully searched the area and came up with a small bag of silver nuggets that had been carelessly dropped into the mud by the pond. Either the outlaws had not noticed in their hurry to make off with the rest of their treasure trove or such a small amount was beneath their dignity to pick up and clean off.

Slocum wiped off the mud and tucked the small leather bag into his pocket. He circled the pond and found no evidence anyone had ever been here, but after almost a month that was not surprising. The hot sun, the restless wind, the waves caused by sun and wind moving tirelessly along the banks all erased details. It had been long enough for everything to be erased.

Looking up at this thought, Slocum hunted in the clear blue sky for circling buzzards. But any bodies would have been picked clean within days. Slocum dropped to one knee, cupped his hands and got some water into his parched mouth. The water was sweet and went down good. He returned to where his mare still grazed. She tried to jerk free when he took her from her small repast, then had to fight the horse to get her away from the water when she began guzzling down gallons.

"You go back to eating," Slocum said, seeing the horse was more inclined to drink until she bloated. He made sure the reins were securely fastened to a low branch.

As he cinched the leather tight, he saw a boot poking out from behind a nearby bush.

Slocum had found the stagecoach driver, or what remained after the ants and coyotes had feasted. The man's pockets had been ripped off as the road agents hurriedly searched for any coin or greenback that might have been tucked away. Anger mounting at Gunnison and anyone else capable of such savagery, Slocum began searching the area in earnest. It took more than an hour to find the other bodies in a ravine almost a hundred yards away.

Two men had been gunned down, but the third corpse caused Slocum's lip to curl in a snarl of anger.

One leg was missing. From the gnaw marks on the remaining bones, Slocum figured the coyotes had fought over this body. Maybe they had even dragged it away. He couldn't tell. For all that, he could not tell who the man had been due to the decomposed condition. As with the driver, the pockets had been ripped off as the road agents hunted for every possible coin.

Slocum took out the watch he had bought from the Paiute and looked at it, wondering if the skeletal body at his feet might once have carried this timepiece. The watch spun slowly in the sun, casting rays in a wide circle. Slocum tucked the watch back in his pocket and knelt to examine the remains.

He flipped open the coat and paused. A single bullet had drilled through the man's heart, causing a rush of blood that soaked a package of papers in a pocket. Slocum pried the papers loose and carefully separated them. Parts of the paper broke off, but the section left told the story.

Slocum had in his hand the unsigned deed to the Digging Fool Saloon. He looked at the body again and knew he could never identify it as that of Peter Halliburton.

But in his gut he knew he had found Starr's husband. Or what was left of him.

10

Slocum leaned back against the largest of the cotton-woods, appreciating its shade as much as he could in the hottest part of the day. He had buried the driver, the two passengers and Peter Halliburton and was tuckered out. His mare ate contentedly at yet another thin patch of grass, oblivious to everything else in the world.

Slocum wished he could be as carefree, but he couldn't. He had to ride back to Hard Rock and tell Starr her husband was dead. Pulling out the sheaf of bloodstained papers, he held them up and read over them, as if this might give him some reason not to return to the mining town and the grieving widow.

The only consolation Slocum found in the whole matter was that he had not slept with a married woman. Starr had been a widow when they had made love. Somehow, though, that didn't make him feel any better or any nobler.

The deed looked to be in order, as much of it as had survived the robbery and murder. All that was needed to get it into Peter Halliburton's name was a single unsigned line showing his mortgage had been paid in full to Jackson Johnson. As it stood, Starr was going to lose the Digging Fool Saloon because the money Halliburton had with him to pay off the loan in Laramie was long gone.

Slocum counted this as another score to settle with Gunnison.

He got to his feet and knew the ride back into town would be a long one for him. He patted his horse's neck and then swung into the saddle.

"She's better off leaving Hard Rock," Slocum told his mare. "So what if she loses the business? The town's dying. It won't be much longer before the silver mines play out and everyone moves on. The saloon will be worthless then. She just hasn't seen it like the others who must have run other saloons."

Slocum worked it out in his head. Starr could pocket whatever revenue the Digging Fool took in, then leave Hard Rock to find a better place to live. Let Jackson Johnson in Laramie repossess the building and everything in it.

By the time it was turning cooler and the sun had dipped below the horizon, he reached the edge of Hard Rock. It seemed to Slocum all he did was report to the marshal what he had found—and all the marshal ever did was ignore him. He ought to tell Dunlap what he had found out in the desert but decided to go straight for the stagecoach office. If the station manager intended to try to slip another silver shipment past the road agents, he had to know what had happened to the previous one.

Slocum dismounted in front of the office and went to the closed door. He twisted the knob, but the door was locked. Wiping a clean spot on the window, he peered inside. The portly station manager and Marshal Dunlap pored over a map on the table. Slocum rapped sharply on the window but both men motioned irritably for him to leave them alone.

"I found the damned stagecoach!" he shouted. That got their attention. The station manager bustled to the door and opened it a few inches so only his face stuck through.

"What's that? What you say you'd found?" Underhill looked pale at Slocum's claim.

"The other stage. The one held up about a month ago. The one with the silver shipment you thought was a secret."

"Where? What happened?"

"Let me in and I'll tell you."

"No, no," the station manager said hastily. "I'm conducting important business now. Come back in the morning."

"You lost one silver shipment. You want to lose another? I can tell you where you can recover your coach, but the driver, two passengers and Peter Halliburton were murdered."

"Yes, yes, but this requires more on my part than just riding out to see. I have to contact the head office in Laramie."

"What about the reward?"

"In the morning, in the morning, man! Now go. I'm very busy." Underhill slammed the door in Slocum's face. The sound of the locking bolt sliding home sounded like a gunshot. Slocum stepped back and wondered if both men had been out in the sun too long. He had solved a crime, recovered valuable company property and even buried the holdup victims and got nothing but an abrupt dismissal as if none of it mattered.

Slocum reckoned they were going ahead with plans to send out another silver shipment soon. Maybe as soon as in the morning. Because they refused to listen to him, the stagecoach would suffer the same fate as its predecessor. Slocum hoped Gus wouldn't be up in the box driving. As cantankerous as the old geezer was, Slocum had taken a shine to him and didn't wish him any harm.

Slocum sat on the boardwalk in front of the stagecoach office and knew he could keep Gus from getting killed by riding shotgun. If the stage company refused, he could trail the coach and do whatever was necessary to keep the driver and passengers from being shot up.

Like Peter Halliburton, Inky and two other passengers had been.

Slocum got to his feet. He had put off telling Starr the bad news as long as he could. Now it was time to confirm what she had suspected since the stagecoach had gone missing.

He walked with a deliberate stride down to the Digging Fool Saloon, then went inside. The miners were whooping it up, dancing with each other in lieu of women who weren't here. At the back of the main room a fight started and ended as quickly. One man let fly with a haymaker that missed and carried him through the flimsy back wall. The onlookers, including his intended victim, laughed heartily and ordered more drinks.

The barkeep and two waiters worked feverishly to keep up with the demand.

It was a thriving business. Slocum hoped Starr was salting away every nickel because she wasn't going to be proprietrix much longer.

"Where's Starr?" he called to the busy bartender.

"Not here," was all the answer he got.

"You lookin' for Miss Starr?" asked a miner with breath strong enough to knock over a sturdy mule. "Said she was headin' to take a bath. Fancy that."

"Yeah, fancy that, wanting to be clean," Slocum said, pushing past the drunk miner and going up the stairs to Starr's room. He knocked and heard nothing. Rattling the doorknob and getting the lock to pop free got him into the pretty woman's bedroom again.

He had not seen a bathtub here, nor was there a barbershop and bathhouse in Hard Rock that he had seen. Slocum was distracted by a sharp sulfur odor coming from Starr's wardrobe. He remembered then how she had mentioned sulfur pools outside town.

This would be the perfect place for a woman in a roughneck mining town to go bathe—and an explanation for the reek of sulfur on her clothing.

Slocum went down the back stairs and got his horse. The mare refused to give him more than a walk as he headed out of town, but that suited Slocum. He needed time to think how best to tell the woman of her loss. Even with the mare walking slowly, Slocum came on a distinct trail off the main road that lead back into the rocks. The sulfur odor that clung to the air alerted him how close he was to a hot springs.

The darkness was intense but from ahead a pale yellow light shone from behind some rocks. Slocum dismounted and advanced on foot, wiggling between two rocks and coming out into a bowl-shaped area. In the middle a spring bubbled warmly, releasing sulfur fumes into the air. Around the rocky rim he saw faint yellow residue.

And in the middle of the pond splashed Starr Halliburton. She had placed a lantern high on a rock to shine light down on her as she bathed. The sight of the naked, wet woman was enough to make Slocum catch his breath. Seldom had he seen any woman as lovely.

She tossed her head back and got the long chestnut-colored hair away from her oval face. Starr leaned back in the pool, her face rising to the nighttime sky as if she were a wolf and ready to bay. As she arched her back, the twin mounds of her white breasts bobbed to the surface. Slocum found himself responding to her naked beauty, and he did not want to.

Not when he was bringing her news of her husband's death.

"Who's there?" she cried, spotting him. Starr splashed about in the pool, paddling for the far side under her lantern. Halfway there, she stopped and stood. The water lapped around her thighs, removing any doubt Slocum might have had that she bathed buck naked.

"It's me," he said. "Slocum."

"Oh, John, you startled me. You came up so quietly."

"I'm sorry," he said, not sure what he was apologizing for. It could have been for frightening her as much as for the loss of her husband. He was too confused to know.

"No need," she said, slipping back into the water and stroking over to a spot just below where he stood. Her ginger eyes fixed on him and read the message he had to deliver better than his words ever could. Starr swallowed hard. Tears leaked from the corners of her eyes.

"I buried Peter next to the stagecoach driver and the other passengers. If you want to put up a proper marker, we can go out and I'll show you the spot."

"He's really dead?" Her voice was low but carried no shock. If anything, Slocum heard an undercurrent of relief.

"Yes," he said softly. He hunkered down on the rock so he could be closer. The woman's expression was one of pain but not great loss.

"I'm sorry Peter's dead, but I expected it. I steeled myself for the news and when it never came, well, what else could I think other than that he was gone?"

"There's more," Slocum said. "Something you're not telling me."

"Peter and I were married but we weren't . . . married."

"I don't understand."

"We were married, but Peter never performed his husbandly duties. He had lost . . . in the war . . . it was terrible, John. But he was a good man and I loved him, all the same!"

Starr began crying. Somehow, she slithered out of the pool and into Slocum's arms, seeking comfort. He held her until the sobbing died away. She pushed back just a little and stared into his green eyes. Starr's lip trembled, then she moved forward again. This time her lips met his in a light kiss that steadily turned more passionate. All the woman's pent-up desires came flooding out even as Slocum's guilt vanished.

She had been married before, but he had not violated her marriage vows.

He kissed her harder. His hands began moving over her water-slick back, across silky skin and lower, down to the curves of her behind. He cupped her buttocks in his hands and squeezed. She emitted a tiny sound of pure bliss.

"That feels so good, John." The brunette wiggled around so his hand slid into the fleshy canyon between and then even lower, across her nether lips. Slocum felt the slick oils leaking from her interior and knew what she wanted.

She wanted the same thing as he did.

Starr arched her back as Slocum kissed her throat and dipped lower into the fleshy canyon between her breasts. He licked and kissed, then slowly worked his way up to the lust-hardened nipple on her right side. His lips teased and his tongue toyed with the rubbery nub. Starr moaned constantly now, her body tense with need.

"John, I need you now. I feel like a string pulled so tight it's about to break."

He ignored her pleas as he worked his mouth across to her other breast with its hard tip. As he pressed his tongue down hard, he felt her excited heart hammering furiously. Slocum worked lower as Starr wiggled and moved around to accommodate his amorous explorations. He came to her navel. Her belly heaved up and then dropped like waves on a storm-wracked ocean. When his tongue found the tangled patch of nut-brown fleece a few inches lower, Starr let out a gasp and trembled all over.

"Yes, John, no, oh! I want you so!"

He ignored what she said and concentrated on driving away all the pain in her, both body and brain. His tongue worked furiously against her, but the brunette was right about one thing. She wanted more—and so did Slocum. He felt uncomfortably tight in his britches.

"Let me get out of my clothes," he said as Starr bucked and thrashed about. She pushed herself backward into the water with a soft splash. She quickly surfaced, again standing on the shallow bottom. Water droplets ran down her sleek white skin, and just above the water rested the deprived triangular spot where Slocum had been licking just seconds before.

"Hurry," she said.

Slocum discarded his gun belt and kicked free of his boots. The rest of his clothing seemed to vanish like magic as he tore off his shirt and pants and slid into the warm water next to the willing, wanton woman. They came together, arms circling each other's bodies. Starr lifted her leg and curled it around his waist, pulling their crotches tightly together.

Then they sank down into the warm water. Slocum tried not to move too much because he felt like a case of dynamite with the fuse burning furiously only inches away. He wanted to prolong the lovemaking in the warm, hot springs, but Starr would have none of that. She was needy and wanted him.

She used the buoyancy given her by the water to float up, then pulled hard with the leg she had around his waist. Slocum gasped as the warmth of her female sheath completely engulfed his manhood. He lost his balance and flopped over in the water. Coming back to the surface, sputtering for breath, he found they were still intimately locked together.

"Do you like this?" she asked breathlessly. The lovely woman didn't appear to move but Slocum felt what she did. It was as if a hand in a velvety glove crushed down powerfully along his entire length. She relaxed and then repeated the thrilling action, using only her inner muscles.

"I like it," he said, kissing her. Their bodies were

pressed together, and the warmth of the water stimulated them as it lapped around intimate areas of their erotically striving bodies. Slocum found himself floating and soaring, being taken completely away by the sensations mounting within.

He knew Starr was ahead of him. She cried out in passion, arched her back and rammed her crotch down into his to take even more of him into her yearning interior. Her trim body trembled and shook, and then her passions died down.

"More," she panted. "I want more of that."

Slocum gave it to her. He cupped her slippery buttocks in his hands and began drawing her to him with firm, insistent tugs. When he was hidden away fully inside her, he began rotating his hips as if he was a spoon and she was a mixing bowl. Only when he felt that he was losing his control did he draw back just enough to remain within her tender pink gates.

He roared back and repeated the actions while he kissed her lips and neck and nibbled at her ears.

All the while, they splashed around in the shallow pool. But Slocum's resolve to continue all night faded when he realized how potent the woman's appeal was to him. Her body fit nicely against his. She used clever sexual tricks on him to rob him of his steely control. Before long he knew he could no longer continue. The fiery heat from his fleshy shaft burned back into his loins and then exploded like a fireball.

As he burst apart, spilling into her hungering cavity, Starr also groaned, gasped and cried out in release again. They rolled over and over in the bubbling water until their passions were spent.

Slocum and Starr sputtered to get the hot, sulfur-laden water from their mouths as they separated. They knelt on the bottom of the slick rock pool so their chins rested on the surface and stared at each other an arm's length apart. Their eyes locked, then their hands reached out so their fingers touched. They drifted closer together with an irresistible attraction and began a new bout of lovemaking.

11

Slocum and Starr stretched out naked on the warm rocks next to the artesian spring–fed pool. He stared up into the night sky, his mind tumbling like a wheel that had come free of its axle. He tried to get the words straight in his mind before he talked to Starr, but somehow every time he started she said something or touched him or otherwise stymied him. Slocum gave up and simply enjoyed the moment of peace.

It felt like the deathly calm before a tornado came whirling through, destroying everything in sight.

Starr rolled over and pressed warmly into him. He stared at her lovely face and wondered what her life had been like coming to Hard Rock. It had not been easy lately and was likely to turn a hell of a lot worse fast.

"You seem so sad, John. Why?"

"I didn't think I'd find Peter alive, but when I saw his corpse, it was still a surprise. I had hoped he was being held by the road agents or—"

"Or that he had thrown in with them?" she finished for him. Her hot breath gusted through the tangled hair on his chest. "Peter wasn't like that. If anything, he was too honest for frontier business doings."

Slocum fumbled and pulled the bloodstained deed to the Digging Fool Saloon out of his pants pocket. He held up it as Starr snuggled around so she could see the sheaf of papers.

"The deed," she said softly. "I've lost the saloon, haven't I? The deed was never signed over to Peter, so he never paid off the loan."

"You can pay and—"

"I can't own the saloon. You know women can't own real estate, even here in Wyoming. Besides, it is such a huge amount. Peter had it all with him."

"You don't think Johnson would give you an extension on the loan?"

She shook her head. The rustle of her brunette hair against his bare skin would have tickled if the matter had not been so serious.

"I have no idea. The bankers stonewalled him when he asked for a loan. Mr. Johnson loaned him the money but under strict conditions of repayment."

"Walk away," Slocum said. "Let the Digging Fool go and get out of town. Hard Rock is dying."

"I know. The others deny it, but the amount of silver mined has been declining for months. Without a new strike, there won't be much left in another few months. But I owe this to Peter's memory. How can I leave it?"

"What would Peter have wanted for you? To stay?"

"I'm the only woman in town after two other saloons went out of business months ago. That ought to have told the miners something. And all the whores left with a traveling medicine show that came through several weeks ago. Professor Smart said he was heading to Denver and the girls could get rich there."

"Richer than here," Slocum said. His mind turned to other things. "What about the new silver shipment?"

"A new one? I hadn't heard," she said. Starr began

running her fingers over Slocum's chest, lightly tracing along old scars as she moved lower.

Slocum's sleeping snake stirred, even after the passion in the hot pool, and he was not adverse to another dalliance with such a beautiful woman, but he had more to show her.

"Take the deed, for whatever it's worth. Johnson will come for the saloon sooner or later." Slocum knew that when Hard Rock dried up and blew away in the hot Wyoming wind, no one would want the saloon. Starr might look at it as not living up to a debt her husband had made, but Slocum saw it as simple self-preservation for the woman. Run the saloon, pocket the money, then leave while the getting was good.

"There's something else you want to show me, isn't there, John?" She giggled like a schoolgirl. "Other than this!" Her fingers wrapped around him and squeezed lightly. He responded, in spite of his determination to finish the disagreeable business of giving her Peter's mementoes.

"Here," he said, pulling out the few items he had taken off Peter Halliburton's body. "If these aren't Peter's . . ."

But they were.

"Here's his watch, too." He passed over the watch he had bought from Limp Foot.

"I'm surprised the road agents didn't steal this, too," she said. Tears formed in her eyes, turning them silvery in the dim night.

Slocum didn't tell her where he had gotten the watch, and he wasn't sure why. Perhaps it was only to keep from complicating matters. Starr had given her husband the watch; Slocum had known that the instant he saw it. She had too much on her plate right now, deciding what to do with the Digging Fool and if she wanted to place a marker on her husband's grave out where he had been murdered.

"You're so good to me. There's no reason for you to

be, and you are. Thank you, John." She kissed him again, and they made love beside the warm pool of water.

Slocum smelled of sulfur, too, when they left, but he didn't care.

Starr had returned to the Digging Fool in time to close it down for the night. Slocum left her counting money and trying to come to a conclusion about finding the lien holder in Laramie or simply leaving with as much money as she could. It pleased him she recognized that Hard Rock's days were numbered, but he was not sure she would take away as much money as she could before Hard Rock became a ghost town. She had an honorable streak in her when it came to taking care of her husband's debts that Slocum admired, even as he knew how impoverishing it might be for her.

Slocum snorted as he walked down the dawn-lit main street. He was a fine one to counsel her to renege on a debt. He sought Limp Foot the Paiute to further question about where he had gotten Peter's watch. Slocum felt honor-bound to settle the score with the road agents for all they had done. He could walk away and no one would care.

Except John Slocum.

A smile crept across his lips. He knew Starr would pay off the debt on the Digging Fool just as he was going to bring down Gunnison, Chettum and the rest of the outlaws. The smile faded when he realized the gang included Jacqueline Renard. He had taken a fancy to the woman during their brief trip from Laramie, but he had seen how involved she was with Gunnison. For all he knew, she was the brains of the gang.

"Limp Foot!" he called, waving when he spotted the Indian at the edge of town. Limp Foot saw him and started hurrying away. Slocum easily caught up with him.

"Whoa, there," Slocum said, grabbing Limp Foot's arm

and pulling him to a halt. "Why are you hightailing it?"

"No want to talk. Dangerous to talk. Dangerous to be seen."

"With you?" Slocum laughed harshly. "I can handle anything that comes my way. Or did you mean *you* would be in danger if anyone saw you talking to *me*?"

"Go away." Limp Foot turned sullen.

"I'll let you be when you tell me where you got the watch I bought off you."

"Found it."

"Like you did the silver jewelry? Which grave did you rob?"

"No rob, no rob!" Limp Foot panicked and tried to pull free. Slocum held him in a steely grip.

"How did you come by the watch? I don't want to know anything else." He fumbled in a vest pocket and pulled out a greenback and held it so Limp Foot could see what it was. "This is yours for telling me."

Limp Foot scowled, then lowered his gaze. Finally, the Indian nodded and motioned for Slocum to come with him. Slocum followed to a ramshackle cabin at the edge of town.

"In there," Limp Foot said. "Find it there."

Slocum opened the door and peered in. Then he was stumbling forward. Limp Foot had shoved him hard enough for him to lose his balance. He tripped over a large rock that had never been removed from the cabin floor and went down heavily. Cursing, Slocum got to his feet and went outside in time to see Limp Foot riding away at a gallop. The Paiute had taken a horse tethered behind the cabin.

Slocum cursed even more volubly, then went to fetch his mare. Limp Foot could never outrun him, but bolting like this only added to Slocum's irritation. He swung into the saddle, got his horse headed after Limp Foot and set off at a brisk walk. There was no reason to kill his horse.

He'd let Limp Foot do that to his cayuse since the Indian galloped at a top speed that could never last more than a few minutes.

Limp Foot proved a more astute rider than Slocum had thought. The Paiute had gone only a few hundred yards out of Hard Rock before leaving the road, and when he had, he worked hard at hiding his trail. Slocum knew the Indian had less than a five-minute head start on him, but Limp Foot used the time to good advantage. Slocum soon found himself riding slower and eventually dismounting to study the sun-baked ground more carefully.

The sun rose above the distant mountains and quickly turned the land into an oven. Slocum used his bandanna to wipe the sweat from his eyes but he kept moving, never giving up. After an hour, his determination had firmed to the point he would follow Limp Foot to the ends of the earth to find out what he wanted.

No matter how Limp Foot doubled back, used bushes to erase his tracks and employed a half-dozen other tricks, Slocum stayed on his trail. By midday Slocum saw that the Paiute was heading toward Ghost Mesa. Somehow, this did not come as much of a surprise. If the Indian had stolen from Gunnison's gang, the mesa top was the place where it had been done.

His mare reared and pawed the air an instant before a gunshot echoed across the desert. Slocum swung into the saddle and pulled down the brim of his hat as he tried to locate the source of the shot sunward of his position.

"Damn," he muttered, seeing what was going on farther along the trail. Slocum put his heels to the mare's flanks. The horse reluctantly obeyed and trotted forward into the middle of real trouble.

The whoops and hollers from the mounted Paiute war party followed Limp Foot like a bad dream. The warriors did not see Slocum streaking forward, head bent low and his horse straining to the utmost. If the Paiutes thought

Limp Foot had looted the graves on Ghost Mesa, they would show him no mercy when they caught up with him.

Slocum had to get to him first—and keep his own scalp.

Rather than eat the Indians' dust, he cut toward the rock spire of Ghost Mesa and found a narrow game trail circling the base. Limp Foot dodged well, feinting one direction and riding the other. The only problem was that his pursuers knew all those tricks and were not thrown off their chase.

They closed the distance inch by inch, second by second until Slocum worried he would get there too late. Then Limp Foot cut back sharply, found a trail up the side of the mesa and shot up it. Slocum doubted the rocky path was large enough to accommodate a man on a horse, and he was right. All Limp Foot wanted was a bit of altitude. His horse launched into the air, soared and landed on the far side of a jagged curtain of rock. Either the Paiutes followed or they backtracked and wasted precious minutes catching up with him.

Slocum saw the first brave try to repeat Limp Foot's desperate jump. The Indian's horse wasn't up to the jump and came down on a rocky needle, the spire impaling it amid loud cries of pain and the death kicks from heavy hooves. The warrior riding the horse was thrown off. When he crashed to the ground at the foot of the rocky wall, he lay unmoving.

The rest of the braves wheeled about and started around rather than trying to follow.

The brief respite from the chase gave Slocum the chance to reach Limp Foot. He was on the same side of the rocky curtain as the panicky Paiute and caught up with him quickly. Limp Foot's horse stumbled and wobbled, exhausted and as frightened as its rider.

"I want to help," Slocum shouted. "We can fight them off together."

"How?"

Slocum had no answer to that because he hadn't thought it through. They had less than five minutes before the increasingly angry Paiutes caught up with them. The only hope Slocum saw was that Limp Foot's pursuers thought they chased a single man without resources. Slocum didn't see that Limp Foot carried either a six-shooter or a rifle.

A few shots might not deter the Paiutes, but it could give added time to find a bolt-hole where they could hide. "We have to hide. Where? Where around here can we hole up?"

Limp Foot pointed to a rugged section near the base of Ghost Mesa. Slocum nodded and indicated the Indian should go to ground while he swung wide. With luck, he could catch the other Paiutes from behind. He didn't cotton much to shooting unsuspecting men in the back, but if it meant keeping Limp Foot alive he could swallow such distaste.

Slocum hit the ground and grabbed his Winchester from the saddle sheath. He saw where Limp Foot worked his way between two boulders and settled down, taking deep breaths to keep his aim from being off. Slocum had only a couple minutes to compose himself before the Paiutes rode up. The leader pointed this way and that, then jabbed his finger directly at the spot where Limp Foot had gone.

Slocum waited until he was sure all the Indians in the hunting party were in view. He fired at the last Paiute, then shifted toward the leader. His first shot took the Indian from the saddle, but his second missed the leader by inches. A piece of eagle feather got shot off from where it was stuck into long black hair, but otherwise he had missed cleanly. The Paiutes' horses bucked and danced about. One Indian was thrown. Slocum winged another.

He didn't understand Paiute but knew the leader tried to rally his men. Slocum got off another shot at the chief, then spun and took out the warrior directly behind him. The leader decided he was up against an army to cause so much damage this fast, and loudly ordered his braves to hightail it.

One picked up the other Slocum had knocked to the ground and then they raced off, doubled up on a single horse. Slocum mopped sweat from his forehead, then hurried to join Limp Foot. He doubted the Paiutes were going to give up the chase because someone had shot a couple of them. If anything, it would make them more determined.

"Come on out," Slocum shouted. "We've got to ride. Fast!"

Limp Foot hobbled out, leading his horse. His eyes were wide.

"You fight for me. Why?"

"I need to know where you got the watch I bought. No more lying."

Limp Foot bowed his head, stared at the ground, then looked up into Slocum's eyes. Slocum knew the Paiute was going to tell the truth. There was a bond between them now, forged in blood.

"I do wrong. I steal my people's grave offerings."

"But not directly?"

Limp Foot shook his head. "I know where the white eyes robbers get things. They rob graves, I rob them."

"On Ghost Mesa?"

Limp Foot nodded.

"Where?"

"There is big path to top. To west. Big trail. Like road where stage rolls." Limp Foot indicated the Hard Rock–Laramie stagecoach road with a jab of his finger.

"Once I get to the top of the mesa, where do I find the white eyes robbers' camp?"

Limp Foot drew a crude map in the dust using his finger. Slocum saw that the entire top of Ghost Mesa was festooned with Paiute graveyards. The one where Gunnison most likely camped was near the middle of the mesa.

"You took the watch from someone there?"

Limp Foot nodded. "Big man. They call him Gunnison."

"Thank you," Slocum said, holding his hand out for Limp Foot to shake. The Paiute blinked in amazement, then smiled and shook his hand. Then he did something that took Slocum by surprise. Limp Foot jerked and pulled Slocum off balance as he swung his left fist. The Paiute hit Slocum on the point of the chin and dropped him to the ground, stunned.

Slocum tried to sit up but could not manage. He flopped back, trying to get his wits back. He heard Limp Foot galloping off. Slocum rolled to his belly, then came to hands and knees. Momentary dizziness hit him, then he was on his feet and rubbing his sore jaw.

"You . . ." Slocum's words trailed off when he saw why Limp Foot had slugged him. "You're one honorable son of a bitch, Limp Foot," Slocum said as a dozen Paiute warriors galloped past as they chased down Limp Foot. The Paiute had saved him from capture and probable death.

Slocum mounted and cautiously rode out of the rocky crevice. He listened hard for galloping horses. All he heard was from off to his right, where the Paiutes chased after Limp Foot. A volley rang out, and Slocum knew his benefactor was dead.

Slocum turned left and rode back to Hard Rock.

12

"The last shipment—the one where Peter rode along—
didn't have any guards," Starr said, a note of anger in her
voice. Slocum stood close to the woman, aware of the
warmth of her body over and above the noonday heat
already boiling off Hard Rock's main street. "He might
not have gone if he had known they were trying to sneak
the silver shipment past the road agents."

Slocum only nodded. He studied the crowd pressing
close to the stagecoach. It was as if everyone had to touch
Old Gus for luck. The stagecoach was filled with armed
guards. Two more rode atop the stage, Meteor 10-gauge
shotguns resting across their laps. Four large strongboxes
filled with silver had been strapped down in the boot. The
station manager pulled down thick leather straps to hold
the boxes in place, then dropped a canvas curtain over the
shipment.

"I hereby deputize all these fine gents. They'll ride to
Laramie as deputy marshals, protectin' the silver and
makin' life a whole lot more profitable for every one of
us!"

A cheer went up at the marshal's fine words. Slocum
was more skeptical. Trying to finesse the shipment past

Gunnison and his gang had not worked, and this ploy would not work, either. The first shot fired at the miners riding as guards would spook them, leaving Gus to fend off the highwaymen by himself.

The silver was going to be stolen if Marshal Dunlap relied on untrained men to guard the treasure shipment. Slocum began thinking of how he could turn what might be a bloody fiasco to his advantage.

"If he had sent this many men out to find the other stage, Peter's body would have been recovered soon after the robbery and m-murder." Starr dabbed at a tear forming, and then straightened.

Her husband's death affected her more than she wanted to show. Starr quieted as she locked her arm through Slocum's. He felt uneasy at this, as much because he didn't want to hurt Starr's reputation as he did by wanting his gun hand free. Studying the crowd revealed a couple cowboys who might be part of Gunnison's gang. Slocum had not gotten a good look at the one Chettum had called Kirk but thought he rode inside the stagecoach compartment. That meant others of the gang might have volunteered to protect the shipment.

"Foxes watching the henhouse," he murmured.

"What's that, John?"

"Nothing. I've got to go talk to an old friend."

"Oh, sorry," Starr said, disengaging her arm. "I hadn't realized I had done that." She smiled weakly, then said softly, "I have to go over the night's receipts and find how much money I really have to pay toward the lien. Will I see you later this afternoon?"

"No promises, but I will try," Slocum said. He listened to Starr with half an ear, his attention increasingly on a figure moving through the crowd near the stagecoach.

"Thank you for everything, John," Starr said, standing on tiptoe and giving him a fleeting kiss on the cheek. She smiled wickedly at him, then hurried into the Digging

Fool Saloon, leaving Slocum free to seek out someone he had never thought to see again this side of hell.

He skirted the crowd, then began pushing into it until he stood immediately behind her.

"A pleasure to see you again, Miss Renard," he said.

Jacqueline Renard jumped as if he had stuck her with a pin. Her hand flashed to the folds of her skirt, then came out without the gun or knife he suspected she had secreted there.

"Why, Mr. Slocum," she said. "I didn't expect to see you again, either. What a . . . pleasant surprise."

Slocum considered asking her straight away where she had disappeared to after sending Clay Chettum to gun him down. The way she acted after recognizing him told Slocum she did not connect him with the man who had spied on Gunnison's camp earlier.

"I looked for you, but then there was that unfortunate avalanche that killed Chettum."

"Why, uh, yes, I suppose. I know nothing of that, you see. I . . . I went off to tend to personal matters and got left in the desert. When I returned to the stagecoach the team was gone and the wagon still had not been repaired."

"You walked a mighty long way into Hard Rock," Slocum said, "but I must admit you look fresh as a daisy."

"I'll take that as a compliment," she said. Jacqueline's nose wrinkled as she looked at him sharply. Slocum knew she scented the sulfur on his skin and clothing from his tryst with Starr Halliburton. Why that put her on guard when sneaking up behind her and scaring her posed a puzzle.

"Let's have lunch. I'm famished, and you must be, also."

"Why is that?"

"It's a mighty long way into Hard Rock, and there's nothing but prickly pear apples and dust to eat along the road. Or hardtack, beans and rice, if you are lucky. How long have you been in town?"

"Oh, I just arrived." She stiffened when he repeated her exact words out on the desert to Gunnison.

"And you look prettier than ever," Slocum said. Jacqueline Renard was scrubbed and clean, had freshly washed clothing and nobody but a fool besotted by her beauty could think she had only arrived after a long trek on foot through the desert.

"Always the Southern gentleman." Jacqueline started to look around, then restrained the urge through force of will. She smiled insincerely and said, "I'd love to get some good food. Do you know anywhere in town?"

"There's one restaurant across the street from the jail," he said, seeing her wince slightly at mention of the hoosegow. "That'll have to do."

They left the throng around the stagecoach. Slocum had not heard when Underhill intended sending out the silver shipment, but he thought it might be soon. If Old Gus pulled out in a couple hours, he could reach a way station twenty miles down the road by sundown. A rest for his team, then continuing on the road at dawn would put him into Laramie by late the next day.

If the road agents didn't strike along the way.

They entered the restaurant.

"It's so nice seeing you again. I had feared you were gone for good," Jacqueline said, as Slocum held the chair out for her to be seated.

"Like Clay Chettum?" Slocum enjoyed needling her but knew he dared not go too far. She was undoubtedly armed and would plug him under the table. Or she might summon Kirk or others from Gunnison's gang to do the job for her. He was not certain what he intended to get from her, but sharing a meal was not likely to give him much information.

"Clay? Was that Mr. Chettum's first name?" Jacqueline smiled sweetly. "I had not known."

"You two seemed to know one another. At least, it sounded that way when you spoke."

"Hardly. We all got on the stage in Laramie, perfect strangers."

They ordered the pot roast with potatoes and exchanged idle chitchat until they were about finished.

"Are you leaving Hard Rock soon, Mr. Slocum? I can't imagine anything that would keep a man like you here for long."

"How do you mean, 'a man like me'?"

"Oh, you don't have the look of a miner or prospector about you. Your occupation seems more . . . violent."

Slocum wondered if she might try recruiting him for the gang. Not for the first time he wondered if Jacqueline Renard might not be the real leader. She had Gunnison wrapped around her little finger, but her control might go further than relaying orders through the outlaw.

"I always try to avoid violence. It's not good for a body's health," he said, finishing the last of his meal. It had been a while since he had eaten this well—or with such a lovely companion. Slocum could not help comparing Jacqueline Renard with Starr.

Jacqueline's dark-haired beauty was striking, but the blue eyes were always cold like chips of ice. Her manner brooked no argument. What she said she meant, and woe to anyone crossing her. Slocum had seen the way Clay Chettum acted. He was a gunman, possibly a good one, and yet had hastily obeyed Jacqueline's every order. Even an owlhoot like Gunnison was reluctant to cross her.

But for all Jacqueline's ice, Slocum felt there was something more to Starr Halliburton. Her softness hid a steel core. Once she decided on something, nothing deterred her. He wasn't sure who was physically more beautiful, but he definitely preferred Starr.

"Sometimes violence can bring you great wealth," Jacqueline said, glancing outside. Slocum followed her gaze and wondered how many of the guards Marshal Dunlap had hired were members of Gunnison's gang. If enough were, the robbery could occur anywhere and would be over fast. A few shots, a couple dead miners and the outlaws would have control of the shipment.

"I've been in town a spell, but I don't recognize some of those gents guarding the stage as being miners," Slocum said, hoping to draw Jacqueline out a mite.

She shrugged her lovely shoulders and smiled. "I wouldn't know."

"What do you know?" he asked, his green eyes locking with her bright blue ones.

"A friend of mine is looking to start a business in town. Perhaps you would like a job working for him."

"Depends on the job and the man," Slocum said.

"The Digging Fool Saloon is going to be sold soon," she said, causing Slocum to perk up his ears. "My friend Mike needs some strong men to keep the order."

"Mike?"

"Mike Gunnison. I doubt you know him," Jacqueline said.

"Big, ugly galoot." Slocum went on to describe what Gunnison had worn during their earlier encounter in the saloon over the poker table. "He tried to cheat me at cards. Is that the way he always does business?"

"Oh, Mr. Slocum. You are so dramatic! Mike would never *cheat* anyone. I am sure it was a misunderstanding."

"I know the rules of poker," Slocum said carefully. He shifted in his seat, hand drifting toward the butt of his Colt Navy. If Jacqueline went for whatever weapon she had hidden in the voluminous folds of her skirt, he wanted to be ready. He saw by her expression she was as likely to kill him now as have Gunnison or Chettum do the chore.

He threatened their scheme, and he was not even sure what that scheme might be, other than to rob every silver shipment they could.

Jacqueline came to a decision, but Slocum did not relax even when it was clear she was not going to gun him down where he sat. The dark-haired woman leaned back, hands folded across her stomach.

"I really must go now. Thank you for the meal, John."

"I hope it won't be our last," he said.

"This is a tough mining town. Who is to say?" Jacqueline Renard stood, nodded politely to him and bustled out of the restaurant. Slocum peeled off a couple greenbacks and left them on the table, following quickly. He wanted to see whom Jacqueline spoke to first.

He had hoped she would go to the members of Gunnison's gang guarding the stagecoach, but she pointedly ignored them and hurried on down the street. Slocum ducked behind a rain barrel, then chanced a quick peek around it. Jacqueline had stopped and waited to see if he had followed her from the restaurant. After almost a full minute she turned, crossed the street and then doubled back. From his vantage point behind the barrel he watched as she walked Hard Rock's main street, alert for any sign she was being followed.

When Jacqueline was convinced he had not bothered, she ducked into the general store. Slocum knew better than to wait for her. He hurried across the street and down an alley between two closely spaced stores in time to see her exit the rear door. The door had not been adequately repaired after Kirk and the others in Gunnison's gang had looted the store. Jacqueline looked up and down the street behind the store, then came directly toward Slocum. He ducked back and pressed hard against the splintery wall of a saddlery store.

Jacqueline walked along briskly, slowing when she got closer. She sniffed once or twice, then looked disgusted at her suspicions and passed Slocum without so much as a glance in his direction. Slocum let out the breath he had been holding. The cloying sulfur odor had almost betrayed him.

Slocum switched sides of the alley and chanced another quick look around. He ducked back fast. Jacqueline and Clay Chettum stood not five paces away.

"You wanted to see me, Jacqueline?" asked Chettum. "You know what Gunnison said. It's kinda dangerous for us to be seen together, leastwise till after the silver's ours."

"Oh, shut up," she snapped. "You were supposed to kill Slocum."

"I did!"

"You bald-faced liar. I just had lunch with him. He is alive and as insufferable as he was on the stagecoach from Laramie."

"He can't be. I cut him down!"

"Shut up, and let me think." Jacqueline tapped her foot as she thought. She finally looked up at Chettum with her cold blue eyes and said, "I won't tell Mike about your failure—if you eliminate Slocum once and for all."

"How do you want me to do it?" asked Chettum.

"Shoot him in the back. You're good at that," she said sarcastically. "Do it soon. I don't want anything going wrong with the robbery this time."

"Nothing went wrong before."

"There weren't supposed to be any passengers, although Mike did get quite a poke off the one fellow," Jacqueline said. "The station manager wouldn't have minded losing a coach and a driver, but he had to report to the main office that he had also lost three passengers. The stage company hates that. We were lucky they didn't send out an army of detectives." Jacqueline fell silent again, then said, "I wonder if Slocum is a company agent."

"If he is and I kill him—"

"Just do it," Jacqueline snapped. "We're in for a passel of trouble no matter who he is, but there's less to worry about if he's dead and buried somewhere."

"Like up on Ghost Mesa?" Chettum laughed at that. Jacqueline did not. She whirled and flounced off amid swishing skirts. Slocum considered taking out Clay Chettum then and there but held back. More went on than he knew, and if he killed Chettum now, he might never learn what it was.

Slocum crept down the alley, then walked more boldly to the Digging Fool. Two miners nursed beers at the bar and gnawed on the free pig's knuckles provided for lunch. He nodded to Leo the barkeep and went up the narrow stairs. The door to Peter Halliburton's office stood ajar. Slocum went and looked in. Starr pored over a ledger book, painstakingly entering numbers into a column.

He almost backed off, not wanting to disturb her, but something gave him away. The brunette looked up. The smile on her face when she recognized him lit up the room.

"John, come in." She closed the ledger and dropped the pen to the desk. "I'm about worn out from all this bookkeeping. I'm glad to see you."

"I've heard Mike Gunnison wants to take over the Digging Fool. Has he approached you with an offer?"

"Gunnison? That obnoxious poker cheat? Why, no, he hasn't. But he wouldn't. He would go to Mr. Johnson over in Laramie if he wanted to buy the saloon. What's going on?"

"A rumor, nothing more," Slocum said. Starr was right. If Gunnison intended to purchase the saloon he would buy it from the lienholder by paying off the loan.

"He might need to ask permission," Starr said, pulling out the sheaf of bloodstained papers Slocum had recovered from her husband's body. "Yes, here it is. I—or Peter—has to be given the chance to pay off the loan before Mr. Johnson can sell it to anyone else. I'm close to having enough, but I need another good week or two."

"Or he might think you own it outright. Starr, let Gunnison have the Digging Fool. Hard Rock is going to dry up and blow away inside a year. Move on. Take the money you have and let Gunnison deal with Johnson when he comes to repossess the saloon."

"Why would a scoundrel like Gunnison want the Digging Fool?" she asked.

Slocum started to answer, then clamped his mouth shut. He had no idea.

"Maybe Gunnison doesn't see that Hard Rock's days are numbered. This might be the last big silver shipment out of town. There's not a mine in the mountains producing more ore than it did even six months ago." Slocum did not believe a word of what he said, because it required Gunnison—and Jacqueline—to be unaware of what was happening in Hard Rock.

"All the miners are saying they are working harder and getting less, but they always say that," Starr pointed out.

"Let the saloon go," he urged.

"No." Starr's refusal was flat and etched in stone. "Peter signed the loan, and it is up to me to repay it. I don't care if I am buying a worthless business. The money has to be repaid. It was loaned in good faith and will be repaid the same way."

This honesty appealed to Slocum, even as he realized it would leave Starr destitute. Still, he had been flat broke and down on his luck more than once and survived. She was a determined lady and would do all right in the long run, too.

"Now," Starr went on. "There's another debt I need to repay."

"What's that?" Slocum asked.

She stood and closed the door, then locked it for privacy. "The one I incurred out at the hot springs. I owe you for all you did." Her eyes locked with his. She grinned and he returned the smile.

"You don't owe me anything," Slocum said. Then Starr began unbuttoning her blouse. She tossed it aside and worked to step free of her long gingham skirt. "Or maybe you do owe me," he said, wanting her more than words could say.

"Then collect it now!" Starr said, coming into his arms and kissing him with fervor.

13

Slocum sat in the corner of the Digging Fool, sipping a shot of whiskey. Starr had told the barkeep to give him the best, but the liquor scorched all the way down to his belly and then burned holes in his gut. He decided it was not a matter of bad tarantula juice as much as the way his thoughts kept wandering. To drink properly, a man had to think about it and appreciate the booze.

He kept wondering about Gunnison wanting to buy the Digging Fool. It made no sense for a road agent to go into business like that. And the men robbing the general store had taken equipment and supplies more in line with providing for a township and not a gang of outlaws. Jacqueline might have wanted decent food rather than the usual trail grub, but Gunnison's men had gone far beyond that.

So many other details failed to make sense, too. He did not doubt Jacqueline had come to town to be sure everything went well when Gunnison's men, posing as guards, robbed the silver shipment. They might as well have been dynamiting fish in a barrel if the deputized miners were not expecting their companions to turn on them.

But why steal the silver and then stick around? Gun-

133

nison was no one's fool, except possibly Jacqueline Renard's. He had to know Hard Rock was running dry. There had to be answers, but Slocum failed to find them as he worked on his drink. What he needed most of all right now was time.

The one thing he didn't have was time. Unless he could buy a day or two.

Slocum knocked back the rest of the fierce amber fluid, shoved his chair back and stepped out into the hot afternoon. The stagecoach with all its guards had been pulled down in front of the stagecoach station. Two men sat on top of the coach, both nodding off in the heat. Two others slept in the shade next to the station. If Slocum wanted to buy himself some time, he had to act now.

He looked around and saw that, like good prairie dogs, the populace had gone down into their burrows for the hottest part of the day. He went to the coach and moved around, dropping to his knees. Slocum wiggled underneath and looked at the way the stagecoach was constructed. Heavy leather straps provided shock absorbers for the passenger compartment. Without some way of taking up the jolts from the rough roads, everyone would end up with chipped teeth—those that had teeth.

Slocum whipped out his thick-bladed knife and began sawing at the leather straps. Four layers supported the compartment. Slocum completely cut through three and halfway through the remaining one on the right front side. He resheathed his knife and swung up to his feet. He dusted himself off and walked around to the front door of the station. From inside he heard Marshal Dunlap arguing with the stationmaster.

"Leave right now," insisted the marshal. "Get a jump on them varmints."

"The horses need another hour or two of rest," insisted Underhill. "We go out with tired horses, they die in the desert."

Slocum opened the door and waited for the two men to notice him. Dunlap turned, looking irritated at the interruption.

"What the hell do you want, Slocum?"

"You know the men you chose for guards, Marshal?"

"What's it to you?"

"I'm still waiting for the reward for finding the other stage," Slocum said. "I don't want to have it held up because you lost this one, too."

"The silver will get delivered in Laramie," Underhill said confidently. He hiked up his belt around his ample paunch and waddled over to his desk. "And I put in for your reward, Slocum. It ought to be authorized on the trip back."

"All the more reason this stagecoach ought to get to Laramie untouched."

"Get on outta here. We got serious business to discuss," the marshal said, shooing Slocum out. Slocum went without another word. He had taken care of the coach. It wouldn't get more than a half mile, jostling and bouncing hard enough to tear through the remaining leather strap. From all Slocum had seen of the men working at this station, it would take a day or two for repairs to be completed.

He had not bought time, he had borrowed it. Now he had to use it the best he could.

Slocum went to the stable, saddled his horse, made sure both he and the mare had enough water, then rode out of Hard Rock in the direction of Ghost Mesa. If answers were to be found anywhere, it was on or around the tower of ragged rock.

The Paiutes rode slowly, rifles shifting restlessly from side to side as they hunted. Slocum sat on a low limb of a cottonwood tree, watching them as silently as a cougar waiting for its prey. He identified the leader of the party by the bullet-broken eagle feather tucked into the man's long black hair. Slocum had shot that feather off the last time they had met.

He hoped the Paiute had never caught sight of him.

His heart rose into his throat as he remembered how Limp Foot had sacrificed himself so Slocum could get away. He felt he owed the Indian something. As much as he owed Starr and her dead husband and even himself.

The band of Indians slowed and formed a tight circle, discussing whatever prey they sought. The leader pointed in the direction they had been traveling, but a younger brave contradicted him.

The chief swung his rifle and caught the brave squarely in the chest, knocking him from horseback. The brave leaped to his feet, shouting what Slocum took to be curses. He ought to let the Paiutes fight it out, but he had other business with them.

Slocum dropped from the tree limb and stood, waiting for the hunters to notice him.

Both the chief and the warrior he had knocked to the ground glanced in his direction. The leader issued a curt order in his own tongue.

Slocum held up his hands to show he wasn't going to shoot. He hoped the Paiutes would do the same since they all had trained their rifles on him.

"I seek a mighty chief of great wisdom. Have I found him?" asked Slocum, looking straight at the leader.

The Indian kicked at his horse's flanks and rode to where he could look down on Slocum. He ignored the brave on the ground entirely.

"Who are you?"

"My name's Slocum. I want to stop those who desecrate the graves of your mighty warriors." He saw how angry mention of the grave robbing made the Paiute.

"Why do you do this?"

"It is wrong. Those who have ridden the Ghost Pony

should be permitted to take their belongings into the Happy Hunting Ground."

"You are white eyes. White eyes steal from our dead," the Paiute leader spat. Slocum stood stock-still. He had to let the chief come to his own conclusions. "Why do you come, if not to steal?"

"I want justice for other wrongs. The same white eyes who steal from your dead have killed my partner." Slocum stretched the truth saying this, but he did not think a long explanation would mean anything to the Paiute leader.

"The ones who rob the noisy coach are those who steal from us," the Paiute said. He glanced over his shoulder and saw the brave he had knocked to the ground was now back on his horse and looking furious. He sneered and turned back to Slocum. "Why should I not let Quick Knife kill you?"

"No reason not to let him try, other than you'd be short a brave. From what I saw, I'd be doing you a favor."

This produced a round of laughter from the other Paiutes and a look of pure rage from Quick Knife. The young brave let out a war cry and bent low as his horse rocketed forward. Because of his goading, Slocum knew this was likely to happen and was ready for the assault.

As Quick Knife reached down to count coup on Slocum with his rifle, Slocum ducked, grabbed and dragged the Indian from his horse. Quick Knife hit the ground hard. Slocum swarmed on top of him, wrenched the Indian's own knife out of his belt and held it to an exposed throat.

"I have no desire to do your work for you," Slocum said, looking at the chief. He got off the fallen Indian and threw the knife into the bushes.

"Stop!" cried the Paiute chief as Quick Knife started for Slocum. "Go back to camp."

"My horse ran off!"

"Walk," the chief said. "Walk or die here." He swung his rifle around and pointed it at the brave. Quick Knife's hatred for his chief was exceeded only by that for Slocum.

Slocum hoped he never crossed paths again with the hot-tempered warrior. The outcome might be entirely different.

"What do you want?" demanded the chief.

"I would return all that has been stolen," Slocum said. "I need to know what is gone from the graves of so many brave warriors."

The Paiute scowled, then said, "Too much to remember. But war club of Fast Tongue is missing."

"Fast Tongue was a great warrior?"

"He was powerful shaman. It is great insult that war club was stolen."

"What does it look like?"

Slocum nodded as the Paiute chief described its silver length studded with bits of turquoise. When the Indian had finished, he stared at Slocum, nodded brusquely, then wheeled about and rode away.

Slocum heaved a deep sigh of relief. He wasn't sure if he had learned anything important, but he had built a bridge to the Paiute chief, if not to his warriors.

Less than a mile outside Hard Rock Slocum saw the marshal arguing with the guards. The stagecoach had broken down.

"Having trouble, Marshal?" called Slocum. He saw his sabotage had worked well. The first big rock in the road had caused enough of a jolt in the stage to break the leather strap he had cut.

"We got to get the stage back. Danged thing broke down." Marshal Dunlap glared at Old Gus, who glared back. Both men seemed to accuse the other of the trouble.

"Can I talk with you a minute, Marshal?" Slocum asked.

"I got troubles, Slocum, that don't include you addin' to 'em." Dunlap kicked at a rock, glared at Gus again, then spat. "What is it, Slocum? Make it quick."

Slocum dismounted and motioned for the marshal to join him a few paces from the stage.

"You know all those men you deputized?" he asked.

"Well, no. I asked for volunteers. Not many men want to take time from draggin' silver outta the ground."

"Ever think some of them might be robbers waiting to get the stage on some deserted stretch of road?"

"And have them rob it then?" Dunlap looked as if the notion had never entered his head. He scratched his chin, then brushed across his mustache before answering. "Might be true, but how can I tell?"

"Which of the men have you seen before? Who are your friends?"

"Ain't got no friends in Hard Rock," Dunlap said.

"Pick the men who have been in town for a spell," Slocum said, taking a different direction. "That fellow on top of the stagecoach. Do you know him? Have you ever seen him in town before you asked for deputies to guard a special shipment to Laramie?" Slocum pointed out Kirk.

"Seen him in the Digging Fool once or twice, but only in the past couple days."

"What about the guy beside him?"

"That's Toothless Joe." Dunlap chuckled. "I was there when his brother hit him in the face with a jar of pickles and knocked three of them teeth out. Why, there was a time when he—"

"You're getting the idea, Marshal," Slocum said. "Fewer might be better on this shipment."

"Yeah, I see what you're gettin at, Slocum. Thanks." Marshal Dunlap hitched up his gun belt and went back to the stage where two men from town worked to get the compartment lifted so they could replace the straps Slocum had slashed.

Slocum swung into the saddle and rode away, aware of Kirk and several others glaring at him. If he stayed in

Hard Rock long enough, he'd have everyone mad at him. Riding toward Ghost Mesa was more dangerous than ever because of what he had done to Quick Knife. Now he had foiled Gunnison's plans for hijacking the silver. Not bad for a day's work.

As he rode toward the Digging Fool, he saw Jacqueline Renard in front of the stagecoach station. She looked surprised at seeing him, then her lips thinned to a line. Slocum tallied up another who wasn't likely to give him so much as a polite greeting.

"How do you do, Miss Renard?" he called as he rode past. Slocum tipped his hat and felt the hair on his neck rising as if someone centered a gun on his back. He was kicking up a real cloud of dust. Now it was time to clear the air enough so he could see a way out for Starr Halliburton.

Slocum tied his horse in the shade beside the saloon, then went into the rickety structure. A couple miners already worked on getting drunk. Most would come in after sundown and a long, backbreaking day of labor in their mines.

"John!" called Starr. She sat at the poker table in the rear of the saloon. He took a beer from the barkeep as he went past and joined the woman.

"You sound cheerful," Slocum said.

"I have enough."

For a moment, he was not sure what she meant. Then he saw the sheet of paper with her careful notations on it.

"You can pay off Johnson over in Laramie?"

"Yes, and still have a few dollars left." Starr sighed. "Not much, barely enough to run the place, but enough."

"Hold off on retiring the mortgage," Slocum advised. "Things are starting to pop."

"I want to get clear of Peter's debts as quickly as I can. The stage just left so I can take the next one in a day or two."

"The stage'll be back," Slocum said, smiling. "Might be a day or two before it heads out."

"Then I can take it."

"No!"

Starr looked at him strangely. "I don't understand, John. You know I am going to pay Mr. Johnson."

"Wait, Starr. There's no need to pay off this week when you can do it next. Use the money and rake in some more."

"What aren't you telling me, John?"

Before Slocum could answer, a hulking Mike Gunnison blocked out the sunlight coming through the door.

"You!" Gunnison bellowed. "I want to talk with you!"

Slocum eased his six-shooter from its holster as the road agent stomped across the saloon, stopped and towered over him.

14

"You have business here?" Slocum asked. He shifted a little so he could fire under the table directly into Gunnison's leg. If the man went for a gun, that would slow him down long enough for Slocum to get his Colt above the top of the table and find a real target—in the road agent's black heart.

"Not with you. With the li'l lady. I want to buy this here saloon."

Starr blinked and started to say something, but no words came out. Slocum realized this was the moment he had been waiting for. More than one problem could be solved.

"The Digging Fool's not for sale." Slocum spoke up before Starr found her voice.

"You her agent?"

"You know women can't own real estate. Of course I'm her agent."

"But, John, I—"

"Starr," Slocum cautioned. He didn't take his eyes off Gunnison. The outlaw shifted his weight from foot to foot, as if he were growing nervous. A jittery outlaw meant a dangerous one. If the lead began flying, Slocum did not want Starr to be in its path.

"I don't care who I talk to, long as I buy the saloon."

"Why don't you start one of your own? Hard Rock's big enough for several," Slocum said.

Gunnison sneered. "Men have tried that and been told it ain't a good idea. Bein' smart fellas, they all moved on real quick."

This gave Slocum pause. Gunnison was as much as admitting that he had driven other saloons out of business or, more likely, prevented men from opening competing gin mills, yet this was the first time he had approached Starr about buying the Digging Fool. As far as Slocum could tell, Gunnison had not recognized Peter Halliburton when he had gunned him down.

"The Digging Fool is a good watering hole," Slocum allowed.

"I want to buy it."

"I'm not—" Starr winced when Slocum kicked her under the table.

"She's not staying in town," Slocum said for her. "What are you offering for the place?"

"John, I have to talk to you," Starr whispered urgently. Slocum ignored her. So did Gunnison.

"Five hundred dollars."

"In greenbacks?"

"Yeah," said Gunnison, knowing paper money was worth half what hard currency was.

"Mrs. Halliburton was just offered a position with a traveling Indian show," Slocum said. "Money's not going to matter much since the show provides room and board, but she needs something different to nail down the position."

"What are you talking about?" Gunnison looked confused. So did Starr.

"A traveling Indian show—a Wild West display is the way its owner bills it—needs more than roping and shooting. Folks like to see real Indian artifacts."

"You want somebody's scalp?"

"Not exactly. I understand the Paiute in these parts have real pretty jewelry. A bag of that, if some of the pieces are unusual enough, might cinch the job for Mrs. Halliburton."

"You'd swap the saloon for a bag of Injun baubles? That's about the dumbest thing I ever heard." Gunnison stared open-mouthed at Slocum's ridiculous offer.

"Not if some of the pieces are unique. Like a silver war club. People back East would pay big money to see something like that."

The words had hardly left Slocum's lips when Gunnison reared back in suspicion. Slocum knew the outlaw had the stolen Paiute war club then, and Gunnison was beginning to wonder how Slocum knew that.

"I might know how to get something like that. You're sayin' a straight swap if I fork over this war club and some other trinkets?"

"If there's enough of them. They have to be silver, too. We wouldn't want to cheat people who paid good money to see genuine Indian trinkets."

"Sure, what else?" Gunnison's pig eyes bored into Slocum, then he nodded abruptly. "Sounds good. Lemme see what I can find. I'll be back to take possession of *my* saloon."

Gunnison left as noisily as he had entered. Slocum sagged in relief and returned his Colt Navy to its holster.

"John! How dare you trade my—Peter's—business for Indian gimcracks! No one would ever buy them. And what's this about me joining a traveling show? I would never!"

"Calm down," Slocum urged. "I've done some thinking. Why did Gunnison leave the deed in your husband's pocket?"

"It wasn't worth anything. He stole the money Peter was taking to Laramie, though."

"It *was* worth something, but he didn't realize it. If Gunnison had wanted the saloon without jumping through hoops, all he needed to do was take the deed to Johnson, pay off the loan and get the Digging Fool signed over to him. This Johnson doesn't care who pays the money as long as he gets it."

"I suppose that's true."

"So you sell Gunnison the saloon for the Indian artifacts. You've still got the legal papers."

"What good will they do if Gunnison is running the Digging Fool?" Starr asked in exasperation.

"We can buy some mighty big help if I return the shaman's club to the Paiutes," Slocum said.

"The Indians? Oh, yes, they'll come to town and take the saloon away from Gunnison," she said sarcastically.

"Might not work that way, exactly," Slocum admitted, "but there might be other ways they can help."

"So, you want me to turn over the saloon to Gunnison so you can give the silver trinkets to the Paiutes?" Starr shook her head. "What do I get out of this?"

"If everything works right, you'll still have the Digging Fool, Gunnison and his gang will be behind bars and no one will need worry about the Paiutes attacking."

"What do you get out of all this, John?"

He hesitated, then grinned. "Let's go upstairs."

"Oh? A down payment?" Starr reached out. Her hand brushed along his forearm and then lightly danced across his crotch, bringing to life an area as warm as the hot springs.

"Why not?" he said. Slocum gulped when Starr's fingers tightened and began massaging. Then as quickly as she had begun the delightful torment, she stopped. The brunette pushed back from the table and went to the stairs. She stopped with one foot a step up, her skirt hiked so he could see the bare ankle and leg above it.

"I'm not wearing anything underneath," she said softly

so only he could hear. With that, the beautiful woman went up the stairs. She stopped again at the top. This time she hiked her skirts high behind her like a frisky can-can dancer to show Slocum she had not been lying. He heaved a deep breath of anticipation and followed.

The sun might be shining outside but inside he had been treated to a delightful view of a full white moon.

As fast as Slocum climbed the stairs, Starr proved faster. By the time he reached the door to her bedroom, she was already delightfully naked. She stood beside the bed, half turned so the sunlight slanted in to highlight the curves and valleys of her trim body.

Tiny shadows cast from her already erect nipples crossed her white flesh. Her breasts were firm and so inviting Slocum could hardly restrain himself. He moved to the woman, circled her with his arms and drew her close so he could bury his face between her pillowy mounds.

"Oh, yes, John, so nice. Your mouth feels good there," she said, but Slocum heard a longing in her voice.

He looked up. Her face was framed between her breasts.

"What more do you want?" he asked.

A smile split her face. She reached down and began stripping him of his clothing. When he was as naked as she was, Starr turned, gripped the foot of her bed with both hands and leaned forward. This tightened the flesh of her rump. She spread her stance enough so that her privates opened to Slocum, if he came in from behind.

"This way, John. Do it to me this way."

He stroked up one slender leg. Starr went up on tiptoe so the muscles tensed as he worked past her knee, kissing there, and then stroked over the softness of her inner thigh. He stood slowly, his hands seeking over every square inch of flesh to fondle and touch and pinch that he thought might arouse her further.

When his hand moved between her legs and through

the tangled nest between her legs, he knew he had succeeded. She was damp and ready for him.

"Don't wait, John. Do it now. Now! Oh!" she gasped. A shudder passed through her body as Slocum stepped behind her. The roundness of her ass fit perfectly into his crotch as he positioned himself. Then he levered forward with his hips. Like an arrow finding a bull's-eye, he sank deep into her moist, trembling interior.

Surrounded by her clinging female tunnel, Slocum languished there for a moment before drawing back. They both gasped at the intensity of the feelings racing through their loins. Slocum reached around the woman and cupped her dangling breasts. Squeezing down hard, he shoved his hips forward. The combination of sensations collided in Starr's body and caused her to begin thrashing about.

Slocum held her firmly. Her nipples turned even harder as excited blood pumped into them. He began stroking back and forth faster now. Friction mounted between his iron-hard shaft and her tender recess. He quickly found that Starr's passion was racing out of control. Her hips bucked and rolled, threatening to displace him.

He abandoned his posts at her breasts and wrapped his arms around her hips. His left arm held her in place while his right hand went exploring the deliciously tangled nest of crinkly fleece between her legs. He found the pink scalloped nether lips and ran his finger along them.

"I'm on fire. I'm burning up. Oh, oh, ohhh!" Starr cried.

Slocum hung on for dear life as the woman's body erupted in passionate release. He stayed hidden away, balls deep in her until she released from the fierce grip of climax. Then he began slipping in and out faster and faster. His fingers found a tiny stud hidden between her nether lips and toyed with it. This caused Starr to buck and moan louder with every touch.

The pressure all around his moving piston of flesh worked to rob him of control. The heat in his manhood worked back to his loins and then there was no way to stop. Slocum lost control as he jetted out his fiery seed into her yearning cavity. Somewhere in the midst of the release, he felt Starr jerk and twitch as a new spike of emotion held her body captive.

She sagged slightly, her knees turned to rubber. Starr clung to the edge of the bed, then looked over her shoulder at Slocum.

"That was the best yet," she said.

"It was over too quick," he said.

"Oh? You didn't like it?"

"Consider it practice for the real thing." He turned her around and took her in his arms to kiss her. After a moment, Starr pushed back and looked at him.

"I want more, too, John, but you tuckered me out. For the moment."

"Later?" he asked.

"Definitely," she said, sitting on the edge of the bed. "You have some business dealings to do, also."

"With Gunnison," Slocum said in disgust. It seemed Mike Gunnison intruded at the least opportune times. But once he and his gang were taken care of, Slocum looked forward to uninterrupted time with Starr Halliburton.

"Go now. Do what you have to, and let me rest."

"Get your strength back," he said jokingly. She wore him out, not the other way around. Starr was a gorgeous, sexually demanding, sexually exciting woman.

Slocum dressed and left, thinking he had time for another beer or two before he heard from Gunnison. As he took the last step into the saloon, he saw he was wrong. Gunnison carried a gunnysack that rattled every time he swung it from one shoulder to the other. From the strain it seemed to place on the big man, it had to be heavy.

"Slocum, got the goods. You ready to turn over the saloon?"

"So fast?" Slocum waved for Gunnison to join him at

the back table where Starr conducted her business. He sat, still wary of the road agent. No trick was beneath a man like Mike Gunnison.

Slocum's eyes widened when he saw the loot dropped on the table. Rings, bracelets, necklaces of intricate design—and a heavy silver stick eighteen inches long studded with blue-green stones. Strange markings cut into the soft silver might have been Paiute holy symbols.

"Sign over the saloon," Gunnison said. "You got what the lady wanted for her traveling medicine show."

"Wild West show," Slocum said, distracted by the sheer quantity of the gewgaws.

"Here. This ought to do. I had the clerk at the land office draw it up all legal-like."

Slocum glanced over it and saw from the way it was worded that Gunnison knew nothing about Johnson over in Laramie owning the lien on the Digging Fool. Any document signed without Johnson's approval was worthless. While it was technically fraud to sell something he didn't own, Slocum had done worse in his day.

"This is for Mrs. Halliburton," Slocum said, affixing his signature to the bottom of the document. "Can you give her until the end of the week to clear out her things from upstairs?"

"I'm taking over operations now," Gunnison said. Then he glanced over his shoulder at the doorway. Jacqueline Renard stood there. The instant she knew Slocum had spotted her, she ducked away. Gunnison shrugged and tried to look as if he had come up with the idea on his own when he said, "Let her stay on till the end of the week. She can run the place, but I get all the profits. And I *will* check to be sure she ain't cheatin' me none."

"Agreed," Slocum said, sliding the worthless document across the table to Gunnison. The outlaw left, laughing and boasting to anyone within hearing how he was now the Digging Fool's owner.

Slocum opened the gunnysack on the table and stared at the silver jewelry. It wasn't worth anything to anyone but a Paiute unless it was melted down—and that had probably been Gunnison's idea when he saw it—but to the Indians it was priceless.

Especially the shaman's stick.

Slocum heaved the sack over his shoulder and decided there was no time like the present to return the loot to the Paiute chief. The sooner peace was declared between the Indians and the white men, the sooner Slocum could concentrate on Gunnison and his gang.

Slocum went to the livery, wondering if he ought to take along a pack animal for the heavy sack. As he worked to saddle his mare, he felt a sudden breeze blow through the stables.

He stepped out of the stall and saw a man silhouetted by the afternoon sun in the doorway. Slocum wondered what kind of a fool would strike a pose like he was going to throw down and yet present himself as such a perfect target. Then he found out.

"Slocum!" shouted Clay Chettum. "I'm here to kill you!"

15

"Did she send you to do her dirty work again?" Slocum said, moving to one side so he could get a better shot at Chettum.

"Who you talkin' 'bout?"

"Jacqueline," Slocum said. "Or does she make you call her Miss Renard, like you are her servant?"

"You son of a bitch," cried Chettum.

Slocum had the man outlined in the door—and then he didn't. Chettum wasn't as foolish as he first appeared. He must have known Slocum would not shoot him down the instant he declared himself. Now Slocum's eyes were blinded by the bright sunlight outside and could not find the dark, fast-moving Chettum inside the dim livery stable.

With a smooth, fast action, Slocum had his hogleg out and firing where he thought Chettum went. He heard his slugs rip through wood. None produced a grunt of pain from his foe.

Realizing he had missed completely with his first three rounds, Slocum ducked, twisted hard and dived into the stall next to his mare. A whine of hot lead told him he had barely reacted in time. He wiggled forward, sat up, then listened hard. His eyes were still a little dazzled by the bright light from outside; it would take a minute or two for him to stop seeing the dancing yellow and blue dots that hindered his aim. A rustle from a couple stalls over told him Chettum was making his move.

Slocum was ready for him.

The shootist leaped into view, his six-gun blazing. Slocum fired directly into Chettum's belly as a bullet creased his leg. Slocum yelped more in surprise than pain, but Clay Chettum doubled over and crashed headfirst to the ground. He twitched and rolled onto his side, kicking hard to swing himself around. His gun hand seemed paralyzed, and he had to move his body rather than the arm when he aimed.

Slocum fired again. This time the slug ripped into the center of Chettum's chest.

"You sonuva . . ." Chettum's words trailed off as life drained from his body. He kicked feebly a final time and then lay still. Slocum got to his feet, limping as he advanced on the fallen gunman. He kicked Chettum's six-gun away and then checked the body. Slocum had cut down enough men in his day to know when he winged them and when he killed them. Chettum was dead.

"Good riddance," Slocum said, shoving his Colt back into the cross-draw holster, then tended to the wound on his leg. It burned like fire but it bled freely, so infection was not likely to set in. Slocum found a clean cloth in his saddlebags, then set to work binding his leg so he could stand on it.

A jolt of pain told him not to run any foot races. Otherwise, he was in good shape and certainly better off than Clay Chettum. Flies had begun buzzing around the corpse and settling on the man's flaccid face.

Slocum knew he had let his enthusiasm for his scheme get the better of him. Mike Gunnison had no reason to turn over so much valuable silver as easily as he had done unless he thought he would get it back. Gunnison would claim the Digging Fool, and Chettum would cut down Slocum and take back the Indian jewelry. With Slocum's body buried somewhere out on the desert, everyone—including Starr—would think he had taken the loot for himself and ridden on.

It worked out nice, except Slocum had not meekly taken a bullet. He dragged Chettum's body into a stall and covered it with straw to keep it from being spotted too soon. Slocum wanted a decent head start before Marshal Dunlap came after him.

Slocum smiled without humor. It might be that Dunlap would never bother looking into Chettum's death, unless he was prodded by Gunnison or sweet-talked into it by Jacqueline Renard. The lawman was not too aggressive about his job, despite what Starr said about Dunlap not cottoning much to murder in town.

Slocum gentled his flighty mare, saddled and mounted. He experienced a twinge in his leg where Chettum had creased him, and then it faded to a dull ache. Slocum leaned back and settled the gunnysack over the horse's rump and then headed out into the hot, dry afternoon to find the Paiutes.

The small fire crackled and popped as Slocum poked it. He had returned to the small stand of cottonwoods where he had spoken last to the Paiute leader. Rather than track down what would probably amount to a speck of dust in a sandstorm, Slocum decided to let the Indians come to him.

He had placed the silver from the burlap sack on a fallen log. The fire cast dancing shadows across the necklaces and bracelets, then shifted and lit them like the very sun. He looked at the silver with some appreciation. The treasure trove was hard to resist. Slocum knew why Gunnison had looted the Indian graves to get it, even if the grave robbing had been worse than outright theft from the stagecoach company.

No one should desecrate a grave, not for silver, not for any reason.

Slocum looked up. He had heard only the faint whisper of wind through the cottonwood leaves but now the *slip-slip-slip* of moccasins on the ground became apparent.

"Good evening," Slocum said, poking the fire higher. The flare caught the flat planes of the Paiute chief's face. The man looked from Slocum to the silver gimcracks on the log.

"What of club?" asked the Paiute.

"This?" Slocum had held it back, keeping the shaman's silver rod in the bag so he could draw it out with a flourish. It glinted in the firelight and caught the Paiute's full attention.

"Give to me!"

"It's yours," Slocum said, holding it out so the Paiute could take it. "Your people's." He sank back down on his heels, staring into the fire and saying nothing more. When the Indian had something more to say, he would. Rushing the conversation was considered rude.

"Why?" the Paiute finally asked. He sat cross-legged across the fire from Slocum.

"Why did I return your property? It is wrong that anyone should steal it."

"White eyes could be rich."

"It isn't right to steal from the dead," Slocum said firmly. "What are you going to do with the jewelry now that you have it back?"

"Return it to graves."

Slocum nodded, then said, "Gunnison and his gang of outlaws will dig up the silver again unless you stop him."

"You hate him so?"

If the Paiutes killed Gunnison, it simplified everything for Slocum. The only part that bothered him was what the

Indians would do to Jacqueline Renard, should they catch her. Slocum pushed that out of his mind. She had put in with vermin and would have to take her medicine for that indiscretion.

"We are not friends," Slocum said, not wanting to go into the reasons for wanting to get rid of Gunnison. "That does not matter. You have your property back—the property belonging to your dead."

"They camp up there." The Paiute chief jerked his thumb skyward. Slocum followed the motion involuntarily, not sure what the warrior meant. Then he realized the Indian pointed to the top of Ghost Mesa.

"May I go there after Gunnison and his followers?"

This struck the Paiute as funny. He laughed.

"You *ask*?"

"That is your people's burial ground. Is it all right for me to go there if I do nothing but hunt Gunnison?"

The Paiute nodded once, sharply, decisively. Then he motioned. From the darkness came a half dozen braves Slocum had suspected of being there but had not spotted. With them strutted Quick Knife. The brave showed his belligerence toward Slocum but said nothing and made no move that would have required a showdown. The Indians gathered the silver, letting their chief reverently carry the shaman's rod.

"We kill if we find. You kill if you find." The Indian looked hard at Slocum, then added, "He is dangerous man, hard to kill." With that, the Paiute leader disappeared into the night.

Slocum strained to hear their footsteps. He didn't. In a few minutes the thunder of horses' hooves hammering against the rocky ground reached him. The Paiutes were gone, taking their legacy with them. Slocum waited a few more minutes, then kicked dirt on the fire and returned to Hard Rock.

* * *

He got back into town a little after midnight. The Digging Fool Saloon was lit and the sounds of laughter from inside told Slocum the miners were enjoying themselves. From the look of the few passed out in front of the saloon, they were doing more than that.

Slocum poked his head inside and saw Mike Gunnison seated on a chair atop the bar like some kind of mining town king. He directed the men dancing on the floor, rewarding them with free liquor if they pleased him. From the number of drunks inside, Slocum guessed most of the men were doing a good job of entertaining Gunnison.

Still, the outlaw wasn't supposed to have taken over control of the Digging Fool until the end of the week. Slocum went around to the rear and quickly climbed the back steps. He pressed his ear against the thin door. Hearing nothing but the tumult from down in the saloon, he slipped into the narrow hall and stood in front of Starr's room.

He knocked and got no answer. Slocum opened the unlocked door and peered in. All of Starr's belongings had been removed, leaving the room bare of everything but the furniture. He checked the other room she had used as an office. Like her bedroom, it, too, had been vacated. Slocum heaved a sigh and wondered where he would find her. He doubted Gunnison—or Jacqueline Renard—had been any too gentle evicting her early.

Although he had not expected them to take over this fast, it did not surprise him unduly. But where had Starr gone?

Slocum went to the far end of town and slowly walked down the street, hunting for any sign of the woman. A smile crossed his face when he saw a light burning in the stables. He looked in and saw Starr sitting on a keg of nails beside a table made from half a rain barrel.

"John!" she cried, running to him. She threw her arms around his neck and held him tight.

"I'm glad to find you. I worried Gunnison might have . . . driven you off." He had started to say "killed you," but caught himself at the last instant.

"He is a horrible man. He and that blue-eyed hussy of his came in and demanded, positively *demanded*, that I leave. I saw no way to prevent them from taking over the operation so I left and came here." Starr looked around almost wistfully. "I didn't have anywhere else to go."

"This is fine, because you'll be back in the Digging Fool before you know it." Slocum went on to explain how the Paiutes would be on the lookout for Gunnison, even if they had not stopped him from rifling the graves on Ghost Mesa.

"I don't see what you'll do to get rid of him. He's been buying up all the town. In another few weeks, he will own Hard Rock."

Slocum wondered at Gunnison's plan—or, more likely, Jacqueline Renard's. Why buy up the town when it was on its last legs? If a year's worth of low-grade silver remained in the hills, it would be a surprise.

"I want to see what Marshal Dunlap has to say about the silver shipment. That might be our chance to catch Gunnison red-handed."

"The marshal is in the saloon," Starr said. "Right after Gunnison threw open the doors and announced free drinks for everyone for an hour, he bellied up to the bar."

"I can imagine," Slocum said, beginning to worry. "What about the station manager?"

"Underhill doesn't drink, so I doubt if he would be there whooping it up on Gunnison's dime."

"I'll be back soon," he promised. Slocum hesitated when he passed the stall where he had left Clay Chettum's body earlier. Without Starr noticing, he poked at the straw. To his relief, the body had been removed.

"Hurry back," she said, looking forlorn. "I'm not sure the horses will provide much company for me tonight."

"I hope not," Slocum said, laughing.

Slocum went to the Digging Fool and entered, keeping his back to the wall as he made his way around the large room. As Starr had said, Marshal Dunlap was at the bar next to Mike Gunnison. She had also been right describing the lawman's condition. Never had Slocum seen a man so drunk and still standing.

If he could call the way Dunlap used both elbows and occasionally his chin on the bar to keep from falling down "still standing."

"Yesh-ir, th-thass right," the marshal slurred. He looked up at Gunnison sitting on his thronelike chair. "Got the damn stagecoach fixed. But there's a she-se-secret."

"What might that be, Marshal? Here, have some more!" Gunnison poured the marshal a stiff jolt from a bottle that might actually have had real whiskey in it. Slocum wanted to call out and tell the marshal to keep his tater trap shut. But it was too late.

"The stationmaster's got a young ar-army of armed agents meetin' the stage 'bout halfway. We get it that far, then it's them Laramie boys's pr-problem."

Slocum saw the cunning look on Gunnison's face. This sealed the fate of the silver shipment. For a brief while, getting rid of Gunnison's gang members and assigning only those miners Dunlap knew personally had been a workable way of protecting the silver. Added to that was the army of agents from Laramie.

Those small advantages evaporated like dew in the hot desert sun now that Gunnison knew the stagecoach company's plan.

16

"Let Gunnison take the silver, John," urged Starr, lying next to him in the stall. She snuggled closer. "If the marshal can't stop him with an entire posse, how can you do it alone?"

"I could set the Paiutes on Gunnison's trail," Slocum said, thinking out loud. He found it hard to concentrate with the woman's fingers slowly drawing curlicues on his bare chest.

"You had a plan," she reminded him. "Carry it out, and Gunnison will go away. That's right, isn't it? That's why you had me give him the saloon."

He knew Starr worried about getting the Digging Fool back. And even if she did not, she intended to pay off Peter's debt. That would leave her well nigh broke and with no saloon to show for it. Slocum could not stop her from doing what she felt was her honor-bound duty, but he wanted to be sure she got something out of it.

The problem he had was figuring out Gunnison's plans. Or Jacqueline Renard's. Why did the outlaw leader want to buy businesses in Hard Rock when the town was dying? He used the silver he stole to buy those very businesses. It made no sense to Slocum because Gunnison was already king of the hill, raiding at will because Marshal Dunlap was afraid of him, and the Paiutes could not catch him, as much as they wanted to because of the way he plundered their cemeteries. Lording it over a few more miners because he owned a saloon might give him a moment of thrill, but that was all.

"I can telegraph the stagecoach office in Laramie and let them know," Slocum said. He wondered why he had not thought of that earlier, then he knew. The reason was her warm hand resting on his bare chest. "If their agents actually arrive in Hard Rock to escort the shipment, Gunnison will have a real fight on his hands if he wants to rob the stage."

"The telegraph line is down, John," Starr said. "I tried to wire Mr. Johnson last night and couldn't."

"Gunnison is a thorough bastard," Slocum grumbled. He sat upright when he heard the uproar outside. He looked at Starr and knew he had lingered too long.

"John, wait," she said. Her fingers gripped hard on his arm. "There's nothing you can do."

"The stagecoach is leaving ahead of schedule. Those men are going to their deaths because the marshal shot off his mouth to the wrong man."

"It hardly matters if Gunnison knew the company agents were on the way. He would still rob the shipment."

"They might have caught him. He knows now he has to strike quick, before the stage meets up with them. The deputized miners riding along as guards are all going to be killed. I should have warned Old Gus last night!"

Slocum shot to his feet and rapidly dressed. His mind raced. He had whiled away the night with Starr rather than alerting the station manager or the stage driver. There was no use crying over spilt milk. He had to stop the stage from leaving or at least slow it to give the company posse time to get to Hard Rock.

Strapping on his six-shooter, Slocum settled the weight

on his hips and then hurried outside into the chilly dawn. His heart sank when he saw how late he was. The coach already clanked and rattled away toward Laramie. His earlier sabotage had been repaired and the chance to do that again had been taken away when Underhill had set a guard to watch over both the stage and the horses.

"You look frazzled, Slocum. What's wrong? A bad night in the hay?" asked Marshal Dunlap.

"You fool," snarled Slocum. "You told Gunnison about the company agents coming to escort the silver shipment. You might as well have signed death warrants for the men guarding the stage!"

Dunlap blinked and shook his head. "I don't know what you're talkin' about. I tied one on last night, but I never . . ."

Slocum knew the marshal had blacked out from too much booze and that it accomplished nothing arguing with him.

"Get a posse together and go after the stage. Gunnison will kill every last one if you don't."

"The silver," mumbled Dunlap. "I didn't know he was a road agent. Why, he done bought the Digging Fool. But you know that. What robber buys a saloon? You gotta be wrong about him."

Slocum stalked off in disgust. The marshal could deny Gunnison's real occupation all he wanted. That would not make Gus and the others any safer when the outlaws struck.

"What's happening, John?" asked Starr, finishing buttoning her blouse.

"I've got to stop the stage before Gunnison," Slocum said. He damned himself for having spent the night with Starr when he ought to have been doing what he could to keep the untrained deputies safe. They would be alert for a robbery, but they were only miners, more used to using picks and dynamite than shotguns and rifles. Slocum suspected they would toss down their rifles at the first shot, foolishly believing Gunnison would not cold-bloodedly murder them.

Slocum remembered what had happened to the earlier stagecoach. The sight of Peter Halliburton's body—or what remained of it—would haunt him forever. Gunnison thought nothing of robbing graves. He would give no quarter to the living.

"What of the saloon, John? What should I do?" Starr rested her hand on his leg. He kept from wincing. She had inadvertently found the bullet wound. Slocum used the pain to focus himself.

"Contact Johnson when you can and tell him you won't pay him until he evicts a squatter in the saloon. Let him earn his money."

"But you sold it, John. You took the Indian silver. That—"

"Don't tell Johnson any of that. If it comes up, you don't know anything about the deal I made with Gunnison. But no one is going to ask."

Slocum saddled his mare and got the horse out into the building heat. He wished he was in the high country. Any high country anywhere else. He got the mare into a trot, wishing he could gallop after the stage. To have done so would have exhausted his mount before he overtook the silver shipment.

He closed his eyes and swallowed hard when he heard distant gunfire. It reminded him of a battleground. The echoes never stopped rolling over the desert. One report followed another until he wondered if the war had really ended. Slocum heaved a deep breath, pulled out his rifle and put his heels to his horse's flanks. The horse had done well so far. Now it balked, trying to throw him. Slocum fought the mare and got her headed back down the road, but not at the gallop he wanted.

By the time he reached the spot where the robbery had

occurred, he was too late. Old Gus hung as limp as a rag doll over the side of the driver's box. Two miners with shiny new handmade stars on their chests stared sightlessly at the clear, cloudless, blue Wyoming sky. Another deputy inside the coach had been filled with so many holes, he leaked blood into a dozen pools. Slocum checked the man, but he was dead.

Riding around to the rear of the stagecoach, he saw where the strongboxes with the silver had been ripped out and lugged off.

The thunder of approaching hooves brought Slocum up from studying the tracks of the retreating road agents. He leveled his rifle, then lowered it when he saw the duster-clad lead rider and the circular badge pinned on his chest.

"You're too late," Slocum called. "You the company agent come to protect the shipment?"

"Reckon we didn't do much of a job," the leader said, riding over to Slocum and eyeing him closely. "Who are you?"

"I came out from Hard Rock and heard the gunshots. Thought I could help, but . . ." Slocum turned bleak eyes to the bodies.

"We heard the gunfire, too. You mind lettin' me check that rifle of yours?"

Slocum started to object, then saw how the others with the agent had fanned out. None drew his six-gun but all watched him like a hungry snake eyes a bird. He silently passed over the rifle. The agent checked it and tossed it back.

"You want to see my six-gun, too?"

"Never mind," the agent said. "Sorry, but I have to do what I can to make sure this mess doesn't get worse. My name's North, and me and my boys was sent from Laramie to protect the shipment."

"The silver's gone," called one of the posse from the rear of the stage. "Looks like a passel of road agents lit out in that direction." He pointed toward Ghost Mesa.

"You know the area? You have the look of a tracker." North looked closely at Slocum, as if he still did not trust him fully.

"I do, but you don't want to go up there," Slocum said, his eyes moving from the rocky base to the flat top of the mesa. "There might be a better way to get your silver, rather than fighting off the Paiutes to catch the road agents."

"Paiutes? You sound like you've been out there."

"Here's what I have in mind," Slocum said. "If it works, the outlaws will take you straight to the silver."

The agent shrugged and finally said, "I ain't goin' nowhere anytime soon, so I might as well listen to what you've got to say."

Slocum looked around, feeling like a rabbit in the sights of a very hungry hunter. He looked over at the stage depot where the agent from Laramie argued with the station manager. Finally, Underhill threw up his pudgy hands in defeat. North turned toward Slocum and nodded once, giving him the go-ahead.

Slocum pushed into the Digging Fool Saloon and saw a couple of Gunnison's men inside, carousing after their easy victory snatching the silver shipment. He went to the bar and said in a loud voice, "I'm here to celebrate. Drinks are on me."

He dropped a small, sweat-stained leather bag to the bar. The impact echoed dully and brought immediate silence to the boisterous drinkers.

"That gold you got in that sack?" asked the barkeep, edging closer. "Nothin' else sounds quite like gold."

"I got a big reward—in gold—for returning all the silver that was stolen today. I can afford to be generous to everyone." From the corner of his eye Slocum saw Kirk nudge another of the road agents. The two argued for a few seconds, then fell silent. Kirk sauntered over and elbowed a man away from Slocum so he could talk.

"What do you mean you got a reward?"

"Like I said. A big one was offered for returning the silver stolen today. You did hear about that, didn't you?" Slocum goaded.

"Reckon there was something said," Kirk allowed. "You returned it? How'd you know where the silver was stashed?"

Slocum laughed and knocked back a shot of decent whiskey. He had to hand it to Starr. She knew how to stock a saloon.

"The Paiutes told me. They got downright sick and tired of putting up with grave robbers. I cozied up to them, and there's nothing that goes on around here that they don't see. Especially over near Ghost Mesa." Slocum had no idea where the silver had been hidden, so he tried to suggest as wide an area as possible.

"Why didn't they keep the silver for themselves?" Kirk asked suspiciously. "Injuns'll steal anything not nailed down."

"Silver doesn't mean anything to a living Paiute," Slocum said. For all he knew, this was true. Their silver ornaments were ceremonial—and intended for use in the afterlife. "It meant even less to me when I heard how much *gold* the stage company offered as a reward."

Kirk started to interrogate Slocum further when the station manager came bustling in, looking uneasy to be in such a den of iniquity.

"There you are, Mr. Slocum. I wanted to tell you that the home office has authorized the rest of your reward."

"The rest?" Kirk's eyebrows arched up. He looked down at the bag of gold and then at Underhill. "He's gettin' more?"

"A princely sum, I know, but the home office feels this

is the best way to deter future robberies. Catching a couple of the road agents helped, too."

"What!" Kirk stepped back, his hand going toward his
six-shooter. He stopped only when he realized no one was
making a move on him.

"You gents drink up while I get the rest of my reward,"
Slocum said, taking Underhill's elbow and steering him
out of the saloon.

"Thank you, sir," the portly man said, wiping sweat. "I
am not inclined toward such places of ill repute, although
I am sure Mrs. Halliburton ran a respectable business, as
these things go."

Slocum ignored his moralizing and demanded, "Are the
agents saddled and ready?"

"Why, yes. Mr. North is waiting at the depot with your
horse. How is the mare working out for you? We might
turn more of the teams to saddle horses if . . ."

Slocum left the station manager talking to himself. He
ran behind the depot and jumped into the saddle.

"You were right, Slocum," said North. "The one you
call Kirk lit out like his britches was on fire. Another one
ran with him."

"Let's go," Slocum said. "We have to get there about
the same time they do or Gunnison might move the silver."

Slocum's mare was hard-pressed to keep up with the
fresher horses ridden by the agent and his men, but she
took energy from Slocum's determination and kept on until it became obvious they were heading for Ghost Mesa.

"What do you know of that place?" asked North.

"Gunnison probably has his hideout up there. From the
direction Kirk is heading, I suspect there is a good-sized
trail leading to the top I'd missed before."

"Some folks say it is haunted," North went on, looking
a little pale.

"Paiute graves up there," Slocum said. "Row upon row

in cemeteries all over the top. And Gunnison desecrated them to rob the dead."

"That's plenty good reason for haints to be rovin'," North said.

"You still game to capture the gang?" asked Slocum.

"You'd go on your own, wouldn't you?" North read the answer in Slocum's cold green eyes. "Never let it be said I'm afraid of any man, this side of the grave or beyond." North spoke bravely, but Slocum saw the hesitation in the man's manner. Several of his posse hung back and a couple eventually faded away, not willing to dare the spirits of the dead on the mesa.

Slocum followed Kirk's tracks easily. The fright he had put into the road agent went beyond mere alarm. Kirk was afraid he had lost his share of the silver from the robbery. Greed drove him faster than any willingness to save his leader. That made him careless, and he left a track a blind man could find.

"It's gettin' toward dusk," North observed.

"That's when the ghosts come out," Slocum needled.

"Then we'd better hurry." North snapped his reins and got his horse climbing. The clatter of rocks and the sound of the struggling horses would alert anyone on the mesa. Slocum drew his six-shooter and laid it on his thigh, ready for use, as he neared the summit.

His precaution proved prudent. A bullet ripped past him. Without even realizing he saw the gunman, Slocum lifted his Colt Navy, cocked and fired in one smooth move. The road agent's bullet missed. Slocum's didn't.

"After 'em, boys!" cried North, rallying his men as they came over the mesa rim.

Slocum was glad no more of the posse had turned tail and run because they faced a half-dozen guns. North and his men were up to the task, however, and quickly surrounded the outlaws. The road agents who weren't shot down where they stood eventually realized they had come to the end of the outlaw trail. They dropped their six-guns and raised their hands.

While his men lassoed the bandits, North went poking around in what looked to be the main camp. North let out a shout of glee when he turned over a pile of rocks at the far end of the camp.

"This is it, men. We got the silver back—and then some."

Slocum eyed the loot. North had recovered not only the silver stolen that day but a goodly portion from earlier heists.

"You're gonna get a real reward this time, Slocum, not just a bag of coins to use as bait. Now let's get the hell off this mesa before it gets too dark." North looked around, shivered and got his men and prisoners headed back down the trail toward Hard Rock.

Slocum remained behind, feeling empty. Kirk and his companion had been caught. So had most of the gang— except Mike Gunnison. If his men kept their mouths shut, there wasn't any way North could bring the leader of the road agents to justice.

As he turned his mare's face toward the road, he felt a cold draft on the back of his neck. Slocum turned and saw a ghostly white figure dancing among the distant rocks. Then it vanished, leaving behind only a soft, eerie moan.

He cruelly put his spurs to his mare's flanks in his hurry to leave Ghost Mesa.

17

"Yes, sir, Slocum, you are in line for a big reward," North said. "They've been plaguin' all of Wyoming for months and you helped bring 'em in."

Slocum stared at the crowded cells in the Hard Rock jail and wished there were two more people locked up. Mike Gunnison was down at the Digging Fool, proclaiming his innocence in the face of the arrests, and Jacqueline Renard was with him. They deserved their own spots in jail, if not in hell, for all they had done.

But unless Marshal Dunlap or North could pry a confession from the locked-up road agents that Gunnison was their leader, it was likely the brains behind the gang would never stand trial.

"There are a few loose ends to tie up," Slocum said.

"Look, Slocum," said North, uncomfortable with what he was trying to say. "About the things I said back there. Up there."

"On the mesa," Slocum furnished.

"Yeah, about the mesa. Don't take it as any weakness on my part, will you?"

Slocum remembered how he had felt when he saw the white misty figure floating across the mesa and heard the mournful wail that accompanied it. He shook his head, then thrust out his hand.

"You do fine work, Agent."

North shook his hand and then said, "I'm always on the lookout for good men. We bring in more criminals than any law enforcement agency in Wyoming. If you join up, I can promise you a hard life, lousy food and one hell of a time trackin' down the vermin."

"I'll think on it, North," answered Slocum, knowing the answer. He wasn't cut out to be a company man. If anything, it was more likely that North would be hunting him sooner or later. His past was checkered with enough illegal activities to brighten any marshal's day, should the right wanted poster fall across the lawman's desk.

Slocum left the agent discussing with Dunlap how they could transport the prisoners to Laramie for trial. He stepped into the street and looked around Hard Rock. It seemed smaller now, less animated than before. And uglier. Slocum tried to push aside the feeling that he walked into a bear trap with his eyes wide open. Something ate away at his gut, and it was more than not bringing in Mike Gunnison.

He walked down the middle of the dusty street and stopped in front of the Digging Fool Saloon. The uproar inside showed the miners' thirsty exuberance at being finished with another day's work more than it did any celebration that the road agents had finally been caught. Slocum believed most of the miners suspected Gunnison of being the outlaw leader but said nothing. He was a respectable man, or as respectable as anyone got in Hard Rock, owning businesses all over.

Slocum went into the saloon and pushed through the crowd, hunting for Gunnison. If he couldn't get the owlhoot arrested, he would call him out. A single bullet could settle the matter in a hurry. But Slocum hunted for Gunnison and did not find him.

As Slocum moved toward the back of the large main room, he saw Jacqueline at the head of the stairs. She stared straight at him, her blue eyes filled with venom. Then she whirled and ran away. Slocum took the steps three at a time to reach the top and saw Jacqueline disappear into what had been Starr's bedroom.

"Wait!" he cried. She did not slow down. Slocum ran down the narrow hallway and kicked the door open. If he had opened it normally, he would have died.

Jacqueline's shot went wide when she was startled by the way the door slammed hard against the wall. She didn't have time to cock the pistol and fire a second time. Slocum rushed to her and grabbed her wrist. The dark-haired woman relinquished the gun, seemed to surrender, then kicked Slocum as hard as she could. He recoiled, giving her the chance to grab for a hunting knife on the bed.

She slashed at him wildly until he cocked the pistol he had taken from her and aimed it at her face.

"It'll be messy," was all he said. Her anger faded to the point where she could control herself. She tossed aside the knife and glared at him.

"You ruined it all. I was going to be rich! You ruined it!"

"Too bad people had to die along the way for your scheme," Slocum said.

"It would have worked. Mike got greedy, but so what? After a couple robberies, we had enough."

"Enough for what?" Slocum asked. He still had not figured out the reason Gunnison had bought so many businesses in a dying boomtown.

"I won't tell you. I'm sorry Chettum didn't kill you like I told him. He was a fool."

"You're the brains behind the gang, aren't you?" Slocum asked. "Gunnison isn't the kind to run an operation like this."

"Of course I am, but you'll never prove it. It'll be your word against mine!"

"Not quite," came Marshal Dunlap's quavering voice. "I just heard you confessin' to a whale of a lot of things that are against the law. That ought to be good enough for a judge and jury."

Jacqueline lashed out, trying to claw Slocum's eyes. He caught her wrists and passed her to Dunlap. It was all the marshal could do to hold her.

"Get her locked up, Marshal. You've done a good day's work."

Slocum said it, but it still didn't feel right to him. He found out fast what was wrong.

18

"I don't understand what's goin' on, Slocum," complained Marshal Dunlap. "This here note from Gunnison says he's willin' to trade, but he doesn't say what he's swappin'."

"Isn't it obvious?" Slocum asked, staring past the marshal to the cell where Jacqueline sat with her arms crossed and staring daggers at the others from Gunnison's gang. "He wants to trade Starr Halliburton for her."

"How do you know that? It don't say it in this here note." Dunlap frowned as he worked through the problem. Slocum knew the marshal wasn't the bravest man ever to pin on a star but had not suspected he was so dim. It might be an act to throw him off the trail, but Slocum doubted it. Dunlap was only a miner who saw what he thought was a job easier than grubbing reluctant ore from the bowels of a hole in the ground.

"I looked all over for Starr, and no one's seen her. What few belongings she took from the Digging Fool when Gunnison took over are still at the livery." Slocum did not go into the small details he had deduced. The disarray of those belongings, evidence Starr had put up quite a fight, the trail leading out of town.

Gunnison had kidnapped Starr soon after learning

Jacqueline Renard had been arrested and put in jail with the others in his gang.

"Why don't he ask for the rest of his gang to be let out, if he's their leader, like you say?" Dunlap scratched his chin and looked skeptical.

Slocum could talk endlessly with the marshal but acting fast was the best course of action. Drawing his six-shooter, Slocum swung around and laid the barrel alongside the marshal's head. Dunlap sat down hard on the unswept floor, unconscious. The key ring at his belt yielded the proper key to Jacqueline Renard's cell.

"Ah, you came to your senses," Jacqueline said nastily.

"You're nothing more than trade goods," Slocum said, spinning her around and tying her hands behind her back.

"How am I supposed to ride like this?" she taunted. "Mike won't like it if you deliver damaged goods. What did he do? Kidnap the bitch who owned the saloon?"

"Move." Slocum shoved the dark-haired woman out of the jailhouse. He had to make tracks before the marshal regained his senses. Considering how averse to action Dunlap was, Slocum doubted any action would be taken. Still, he wanted to get on the trail to catch up with Gunnison before he took out his wrath on Starr.

Slocum helped Jacqueline into the saddle of a swaybacked horse at the stable, then mounted his mare and rode from Hard Rock, leading the other horse.

"You've been a real thorn in the ass, Slocum," Jacqueline said. "If you have any sense you and the saloon whore will leave Wyoming as fast as you can ride."

Slocum bit back a retort. He was already angry with himself for not considering how desperate Gunnison would be after his gang and all the loot was taken into custody. The truth was that Slocum had figured on catching Mike Gunnison with the other road agents. When it turned out Gunnison had not been in the outlaw camp atop Ghost Mesa, Slocum ought to have ridden straight for

Hard Rock to gun him down. That would have saved a passel of trouble.

"Where's he likely to be? Up with the spooks on Ghost Mesa?" Slocum saw the way Jacqueline's lip curled into a sneer.

"You afraid of ghosts, Slocum?"

"I've never seen anything that wasn't stopped in its tracks by a well-aimed bullet," he said. "Where's Gunnison likely to have taken Starr?"

"You're right. On the mesa. The Paiutes won't go there, except to bury their dead. They think it's haunted, and who knows that it isn't?"

"Save that for someone who scares easy," Slocum said. He retraced the route taken earlier by North and his posse to the top of Ghost Mesa. Riding in the dark was hard, but the moans and wails he had heard on earlier treks to the mesa were lacking. But Slocum did smell a sharp, pungent sulfur scent reminiscent of the hot springs where he and Starr had whiled away the time so pleasantly.

"What causes the ghost sounds? Releasing steam?" he asked her.

From her reaction he had guessed accurately. Jacqueline turned even angrier and spat like a stepped-on cat.

"Burn in hell, Slocum," she snapped.

Slocum ignored her when he heard faint sounds all around. They rode near the base of the mesa, and he suspected the Paiutes might be flanking him. He hoped the return of the shaman's silver war club bought him safe passage. Fighting the Indians and trying to get Starr free from Gunnison's clutches was one more fight than he needed.

"Mike! He's got me all tied up!" shouted Jacqueline. She must have heard the sounds around them, too.

"Shut up," Slocum said, but he heard sounds from ahead, near the base of the trail going straight to the mesa summit.

He drew his six-gun and held it down by his leg, ready for instant use.

"You brought her. Good," said Mike Gunnison, stepping from the darkness of a cottonwood stand ahead.

Slocum had underestimated Gunnison before. Not this time. He lifted his six-shooter and fired at the man without even answering. The shot winged the outlaw and spun him around.

"You shot me!" Gunnison wailed.

"I missed," Slocum said coldly, firing again at the road agent. No matter what, Slocum knew he was doing the right thing shooting Gunnison. If Gunnison had killed Starr, he deserved no quarter. If he hadn't, this was the best way of freeing the woman.

"Mike!" cried Jacqueline. "Run, kill her, get away!"

Slocum emptied his six-shooter at Gunnison, missing with his last five shots. He shoved the gun into his cross-draw holster and drew out his rifle, but Gunnison had slithered into the brush like a stepped-on rattler.

"John!" came the weak call from a few yards off.

Slocum considered going after Gunnison, then homed in on Starr's voice. He found her tied to a tree. Quickly cutting her ropes, he took her in his arms for a moment, then pushed her away.

"There's no time. I have to get Gunnison." Slocum cocked his head to one side when he heard horse's hooves pounding away.

"He's going up the road to the top of the mesa," Starr said.

Slocum knocked out the cylinder from his Colt Navy and dropped in a fully loaded one before handing the pistol to Starr.

"Keep a sharp eye on Jacqueline. Don't hesitate to shoot her, if you have to."

"I . . . I will."

"She and Gunnison headed the gang that killed Peter,"

Slocum told her, a savage note in his voice to make her more aggressive should the need arise. He didn't even much care if Starr shot Jacqueline down where she stood, though he hoped she would let the outlaw woman stand trial.

"I understand," Starr said.

Before she could say another word, Slocum swung into the saddle and lit out after Gunnison. The road agent made a beeline for the top of Ghost Mesa. Slocum figured the outlaw might have a bolt-hole there where he could hide out until the pursuit stopped.

He did not know John Slocum. Slocum would never stop hunting until he found the outlaw.

The mare protested, but Slocum pushed her hard all the way to the crest of the road. Ghost Mesa stretched out, as silent as a shroud and cloaked in darkness. No sign of Gunnison. Slocum tried to find the man's tracks but the rocky ground had not taken hoofprints, which might have been another reason Gunnison had chosen this for a hideout. Safe from Indians, graves to plunder, a safe place to hide from any posse with a view of the desert floor for miles around—this was an outlaw's perfect lair.

He could not track Gunnison but the whisper and moan from directly ahead, near the center of the mesa, drew Slocum like flies to cow flop. Within a couple hundred yards he knew he was on the right trail. From ahead came the nose-wrinkling sulfur smell of hot springs. If a gang of outlaws had to camp anywhere, it would be near water.

Slocum dismounted when he reached a tumble of rocks. He canted his head to one side. Through the soft whine of wind came scraping sounds of boot leather against stone. He levered a round into the chamber of his Winchester and went hunting.

A path winding through the boulders showed recent use. Slocum saw garbage carelessly tossed aside and knew he had found the outlaws' hideout. He came into a shallow bowl dominated by a large pool of water. The scent of volcanic springs came stronger now, and a hissing sound put Slocum on edge.

He spun, rifle ready to fire when a ghostly white form drifted down toward him. Slocum relaxed when he saw it was only steam from the hot springs. The hot, moist air rose, found cooler rocks and turned to fog that caught a ride on the gentle wind blowing over the pool. He had discovered what made both the ghostly shapes and the mournful wailing.

A new sound alerted Slocum that he was not alone on the edge of the pool. He turned and saw a dark figure moving on the far side of the pond.

"Gunnison!" he yelled.

"How'd you find me? You son of a bitch. You shot me."

A hail of bullets came in Slocum's direction. If he had been sure of his target, Slocum would have fired on Gunnison without quarter. But the dark hid the outlaw—until he opened fire. Slocum traced the foot-long yellow-and-orange flashes from the road agent's six-shooter back to where a hand held the butt. He fired deliberately into the darkness where Gunnison's body had to be.

The first shot caused the robber to grunt. The second and third stopped the return fire. And the fourth bullet from Slocum's trusty Winchester whined into the distance, ricocheting off rock. He cautiously circled the pool until he saw the body on the ground, arms out-flung. Gunnison had dropped his six-gun, but Slocum approached warily.

He kicked the six-shooter away before kneeling to check for life.

Mike Gunnison had cheated the hangman by dying from Slocum's well-aimed slugs.

Slocum considered leaving the outlaw's body for the buzzards, then decided to bury him some distance away from where the Paiutes had interred their braves. Gunnison did not deserve to be in the same ground, but Slocum was not going to haul the corpse back to Hard Rock. After a half hour of backbreaking work, he had the body covered with enough rocks to keep off the buzzards and any coyote looking for a quick meal.

Only then did he turn his back on the wails and moans and shifting white clouds of fog from the venting hot springs.

"Ghost Mesa," Slocum scoffed as he tried to tell himself he had never believed the Indian burial ground was haunted. He rode to the bottom of the trail and turned for the stand of cottonwood trees where he had left Starr guarding Jacqueline Renard.

"Starr!" he called. "Where are you? It's me, Slocum!"

He dismounted and let his horse nibble at some juicy grass. He turned and found himself staring down the barrel of a gun.

Slocum's hand flashed to his Colt Navy, then froze when he found only empty leather. This was not any six-shooter he faced. It was his own. The one he had given Starr to guard Jacqueline Renard.

"She was such a silly goose," Jacqueline said. "She believed me when I said the ropes were too tight on my wrists."

"Starr ought to have shot you down," Slocum said. "I should have."

Jacqueline laughed and it was not pleasant.

"Yes, Slocum, you should have, but you're as soft-hearted as she is."

"Did you kill her?" Slocum felt hollow inside, fearing the answer.

"I kept her alive, in case I needed her to lure you in." Jacqueline motioned with the Colt. Slocum obeyed. He saw that he would die on the spot if he did not go along with whatever scheme Jacqueline had concocted.

"Starr!" Slocum dropped to his knees and pulled the gag from the brunette's mouth. She kept from sobbing.

"Don't bother untying her," Jacqueline said. "It would be a waste of your last minutes of life."

"Silver, John," Starr gasped out. "Gunnison told me, bragged about it. There's a huge vein of silver under Hard Rock! The entire town is sitting on a mother lode of silver!"

"That's why he wanted to buy the businesses," Slocum said.

"The Digging Fool sits on the spot where the vein comes out of the ground, and I never knew. A mining engineer from Laramie found it, but Gunnison killed him before he could return to tell anyone."

"Before he could file mineral rights on the land for himself," Slocum said.

"Can you die happy now, Slocum? That's a shame. I wanted you to suffer before I shot you!" Jacqueline cocked the six-shooter and trained it squarely on him.

Slocum reached for his knife but saw he could never throw it in time. He was in Jacqueline's sights, and her finger tightened on the hair trigger.

Slocum blinked, not sure what he saw. Jacqueline screamed and jerked around violently as if she had stepped into a nest of red ants. She took a step, twisted around, tripped and fell facedown with the gun under her.

The six-shooter discharged when she hit the ground. Her body jerked once, then sagged lifelessly.

Slocum and Starr stared at the floating white wisp that had engulfed Jacqueline Renard for the brief moment before she had reacted so strangely.

The fog assumed a familiar human shape, swirled about in a small tornado that looked like a hand reaching out to them, then vanished on the gentle evening breeze.

"That looked like the Indian who always came to town to beg and steal things," Starr said.

"Limp Foot," Slocum said in a choked voice. "That was Limp Foot saving me. Again."

"I don't understand, John."

"Never mind. I'm not sure I do, either. Let's get back to town. You've got money to send to Johnson in Laramie—and a silver mine to make you rich."

Slocum and Starr headed back to Hard Rock and a fortune.

The buzzard flew high, its ugly head in heaven and its sharp eyes fixed on hell below. It spread its wings wider and wheeled when a blast of rising hot air from the desert gave it some additional lift. It dipped lower as it studied the burning arid terrain for any hint of a decent rotting meal. Barring that, the double-rutted road through the alkali plain sometimes offered up a tasty tidbit waiting to die.

Not today.

The buzzard circled and rode the air currents higher, heading over the nearby steep-sided mesa. Nothing there anymore. The buzzard hunted on, a distant billowing dust cloud catching its sharp gaze. The best source of food it had ever found approached.

Humans. Droves of them rushing to the nearby town in wagons and on horseback.

It would dine. But not today. Eventually. When the town died again.

LONGARM

Explore the exciting Old West with one of the men who made it wild!

__LONGARM AND THE NEVADA NYMPHS #240   0-515-12411-7/$4.99
__LONGARM AND THE COLORADO COUNTERFEITER #241
         0-515-12437-0/$4.99
__LONGARM GIANT #18: LONGARM AND THE DANISH DAMES
         0-515-12435-4/$5.50
__LONGARM AND THE RED-LIGHT LADIES #242   0-515-12450-8/$4.99
__LONGARM AND THE KANSAS JAILBIRD #243   0-515-12468-0/$4.99
__LONGARM AND THE DEVIL'S SISTER #244   0-515-12485-0/$4.99
__LONGARM AND THE VANISHING VIRGIN #245   0-515-12511-3/$4.99
__LONGARM AND THE CURSED CORPSE #246   0-515-12519-9/$4.99
__LONGARM AND THE LADY FROM TOMBSTONE #247
         0-515-12533-4/$4.99
__LONGARM AND THE WRONGED WOMAN #248   0-515-12556-3/$4.99
__LONGARM AND THE SHEEP WAR #249   0-515-12572-5/$4.99
__LONGARM AND THE CHAIN GANG WOMEN #250   0-515-12614-4/$4.99
__LONGARM AND THE DIARY OF MADAME VELVET #251
         0-515-12660-8/$4.99
__LONGARM AND THE FOUR CORNERS GANG #252   0-515-12687-X/$4.99
__LONGARM IN THE VALLEY OF SIN #253   0-515-12707-8/$4.99
__LONGARM AND THE REDHEAD'S RANSOM #254   0-515-12734-5/$4.99
__LONGARM AND THE MUSTANG MAIDEN #255   0-515-12755-8/$4.99
__LONGARM AND THE DYNAMITE DAMSEL #256   0-515-12770-1/$4.99
__LONGARM AND THE NEVADA BELLY DANCER #257   0-515-12790-6/$4.99
__LONGARM AND THE PISTOLERO PRINCESS #258   0-515-12808-2/$4.99